MW00606291

TACTICAL FORCE

TRIUMPH OVER ADVERSITY

LYNN SHANNON

TACTICAL FORCE

Now faith is confidence in what we hope for and assurance about what we do not see.

Hebrews 11:1

ONE

The door was open.

Hayley Barlow paused on the rickety front porch of her mother's house. The sun had set hours ago, dropping a shroud of darkness over the property. A faint glow came from the lone bulb overhead, illuminating the faint crack between the front door and the frame. She'd locked up before leaving. She was sure of it.

Her heart skittered. Hayley's hand automatically drifted to the handgun concealed under her jacket only for her fingers to brush against fabric. Belatedly, she realized her weapon was inside the house, secure in a drawer in the entryway. It was rare she was without it. Being attacked and held prisoner for days by a sadistic killer, along with a career as a military police officer, had embedded the need for protection into her psyche. But wearing the handgun, even in a concealed manner during her mother's funeral, had seemed disrespectful.

Janet Barlow hated guns.

A strange quirk considering her mom had no qualms about breaking the law. Stealing, child endangerment, and drug dealing were just a few of the arrests on her rap sheet. Liquor and pain pills hadn't helped matters. Janet's addiction had ebbed and flowed for decades, finally culminating in her death three days ago. Her funeral and burial had been this afternoon. Hayley was emotionally drained, and now someone had broken into her family's home.

Frigid wind rippled the strands of Hayley's dark hair. The front door creaked on the hinges, opening wider, revealing a dark interior. Was she mistaken about the intruder? Had the wind simply pushed the door open? She frowned, trying to remember. She'd closed the door firmly, but hadn't double-checked it. Maybe the latch hadn't clicked into place.

The ancient farmhouse had been built by her grandfather. It'd been beautiful once, with flower beds lining the walkway and rocking chairs on the wooden porch. Time and vicious thunderstorms had beaten the building into submission. Shingles were missing from the roof and paint peeled from the wood siding. Weeds tangled together, climbing the posts of the porch in an attempt to swallow the house. Hayley almost wished they would. After clearing the farmhouse of her mother's meager belongings, Hayley would put the property up for sale. She never wanted to come back to Knoxville, Texas again.

Too many horrific memories.

An owl hooted. Moonlight slid along the woods surrounding the house and another icy wind snaked into Hayley's jacket. The hair on the back of her neck stood on end. A sense of being watched crept over her. Hayley cast a glance over her shoulder but couldn't distinguish anything unusual in the yard. She slid along the wooden porch to the front door. Gingerly, she pushed open the door with her foot.

Darkness yawned. Boxes were piled neatly in the corner. An old couch sagged against the living room wall across from a fireplace. Somewhere deeper inside the house came a whisper, followed by the scrape of a boot against the floor.

Someone was definitely inside.

Hayley quietly located the key to the console in the entryway and unlocked the first drawer. Wood scraped against wood as she pulled it open, and she winced at the loud noise. Relief flooded her veins when her hand closed over the grip of her handgun. Automatically, she checked to make sure the weapon was loaded. It was.

"This is..." Hayley caught herself before she said military police. She wasn't in the Army anymore. Her career ended six months ago after a bullet ricocheted off concrete and fragments hit her right hand. The injury hadn't been life-threatening, but the bullet had damaged a tendon, which affected her shooting accuracy. Hayley could still handle a weapon, but not with the same precision as before.

Another scrape came from inside the house. Was he in the back bedroom?

"Whoever you are, this is private property." Hayley's voice carried through the home. "You're trespassing and I'm armed. Come out with your hands up."

No response. Chances were, it was some lowlife her mother had hung out with. Hayley debated calling law enforcement, but it would take time for deputies to reach the house. She was out in the boonies. Besides, she couldn't be sure the person didn't have a right to be in the house. Her mother could've given someone a key. A boyfriend, maybe? No one had come to the funeral, but that didn't exclude the possibility.

"Show yourself." Hayley silently moved over the worn wooden floors toward the hallway leading to the back bedrooms. No one responded to her order. She rounded the corner, gun leading the way, and paused. Light flickered from the main bedroom in a warm glow, as if someone had lit a candle. Rose petals were scattered on the threadbare carpet.

Weird. Did the boyfriend not know her mother was dead?

Hayley continued down the hall, carefully clearing the other rooms as she passed. The guest bedroom was empty, as was the small bathroom. She slid up to the doorjamb of the primary bedroom at the end of the hall, her heart beating a rapid tune against her ribs. "I know you're in there. Announce yourself."

No reply. Hayley peeked around the corner.

Rose petals were scattered around the room. Candles lined the dresser. The bed was covered by a handmade quilt, sewn by Hayley's grandmother before she passed. A large heart made out of rosebuds rested on it. The room was set for a romantic interlude.

No boyfriend.

Hayley eased into the bedroom, the heavy scent of the roses mingling with winter air. The curtains fluttered. The window was open. Had the person escaped into the backyard? Possible. But Hayley still had the adjacent bathroom to clear. She wouldn't let down her guard until it was certain the house was empty. She pivoted into the bathroom, pushing aside the shower curtain on the bathtub.

Empty. No one was here.

Hayley released the breath she was holding and lowered her weapon. The cell phone tucked inside her jacket pocket vibrated. She pulled it out. The number flashing across her screen was unfamiliar, but local. She answered the call. "Hello."

"My sweetheart..."

His voice was barely above a whisper, nothing more than a faint echo on the wind, but Hayley stiffened immediately. The roses... the candles... Fear doused her like an ice-water bath. She raised her weapon, pointing it at the bathroom door, which led into the bedroom. Had he snuck in behind her? Hayley's breath hitched. "Who is this?"

"You know exactly who I am."

Casanova? No, it couldn't be the criminal who'd kidnapped and held her for days. Hayley's mind rejected it, even as memories assaulted her senses. The feel of the gun barrel pressed up against her spine when the killer carjacked Hayley and her boyfriend's sister, Lauren. Driving to the woods under the cover of night. Frigid air and the crunch of leaves on the pathway as they were forced to walk after their hands were bound.

The sound of the gunshot that stole Lauren's life. Blood. So much blood.

"It's been a long time." He hummed, the sound coming over the line. "I've missed you."

The voice was the same. Smooth and haunting, with just the barest hint of a Texas accent. The brand on her shoulder burned, the pain as vibrant as it'd been on the day he'd pressed a hot iron to her skin. *You belong to me.* The wound was heart shaped, a constant reminder of the man who'd nearly taken her life. He'd worn an ancient Venetian mask made out of hard plastic with a pointed nose and chin. No mouth. His eyes had been malevolent, cavernous holes. He'd called himself Casanova. She'd never known his true identity.

Law enforcement believed he was dead. There hadn't been any sign of him for ten years.

Until now.

Hayley's hand clutched the cell phone as terror turned to rage. If this was Casanova, he'd made a calculated error. She wasn't the same helpless seventeen-year-old girl he'd carjacked. Now Hayley was a trained military police officer with years of experience under her belt. She eased back into the bedroom. The scent of the roses turned her stomach. "Hiding, Casanova? That's not very manly."

He chuckled. "You can't bait me, sweetheart, but nice try. Do you like the gifts I've left you?"

Hayley slid to the open window. Goose bumps broke out across her skin as frosty air skated over her bare neck. She peered into the woods bordering the property. The trees and brush cast deep shadows. If Casanova was hiding out there, she couldn't tell. "What do you want?"

"You."

A shudder rippled down her spine. Hayley's insides quaked, but she didn't allow an ounce of fear to bleed into her voice. "Then come and get me."

"Soon, sweetheart. Very soon. But I have a game for us to play first. Look at the roses on the bed. I've left instructions."

He hung up. Hayley's breath was uneven, and she didn't move from the window. Her gaze swept the yard and trees once more, but again, nothing stirred. Using the edge of her jacket sleeve to cover her hand, and touching the window as little as possible to preserve potential fingerprints, she shut it. The act didn't make her feel one bit safer.

Heart pounding, she edged closer to the bed. An envelope was tucked between the rosebuds on the quilt. Her name was typed on the front. Hayley didn't immediately touch it. Instead, she went back into the bathroom and fished out a pair of latex gloves from under the sink. She yanked them on before crossing back to the bed. The envelope was plain, sold from hundreds of stationery stores across the country. It was unsealed.

Hayley lifted the flap.

A woman's bracelet fell into her hand.

TWO

Walker Montgomery's heart rate spiked as a set of hooves aimed straight for his head.

He lunged. Wind whispered past as the horse narrowly missed him, landing on the hard packed ground with a snort. The beast was massive, black as coal, with the attitude of an animal who'd been mistreated by humans and had no desire to repeat the experience. The whites of his eyes showed as he whirled away from Walker and raced to the other side of the paddock.

"Was that how it was supposed to go?" Nathan Hollister, Walker's friend, leaned against the fence. He wore dusty cowboy boots, a thick coat, and a smirk. "Cuz old Midnight over there nearly gave you a concussion."

Walker shot him a glare. "Shut up."

Nathan's smirk widened, and he raised his voice to a mocking tone. "No, don't help me. I know what I'm doing. I have the touch. Horses love me." He gaffed. "You've got the touch all right."

Walker kept his voice low to avoid frightening the horse but made sure Nathan caught the arch of his brows as they hiked closer to the cowboy hat shielding his eyes from the late afternoon sun. "I'll give you a touch of my fists."

Nathan snorted. "I'd like to see you try."

The teasing was all bluster. Neither man would ever lay a hand on the other unless they were sparring in the gym. Walker and Nathan were brothers in everything but blood. They'd met two years ago at a local rodeo event. Both were veterans. Different branches— Nathan had been a Green Beret, Walker a Navy SEAL—but their shared service had formed an instant bond that'd deepened over time.

Walker turned his back on his friend and focused on the horse. Midnight was plastered against the other side of the paddock. A lead rope hung from his halter and trailed in the dirt. Whip marks criss-crossed his flanks, stark against his dark coat. Each of the horse's ribs were visible. The poor animal had been beaten and starved by his previous owner but, despite it all, had some spunk left. He was calmer now that there was distance between them.

"What do you think, Cassie?" Walker turned to the woman at his side. Cassie was Nathan's wife. She ran a rescue operation for abused horses. Her stables were full, and she'd called two hours ago begging Walker to take Midnight for a few weeks until there was space on her ranch. "Should I try again?"

Cassie nodded. Her blonde hair was pulled back into a ponytail, a concentrated look etched on her pretty features. "We have to make him comfortable enough for you to approach him. Otherwise, you won't be able to get him into the barn at night." She tilted her head. "Go slow and talk to him in a quiet voice, just like you were doing."

Walker's dog, Boone, barked from his place on the other side of the fence. The hound dog followed it with a whimper, as if warning his master not to approach the horse.

Nathan crouched down next to him, patting Boone on the head. "Don't worry, boy. Cassie won't let anything happen to Walker." Laughter filled his voice. "At least one of them knows what to do with Midnight."

This time, it was Cassie who shot her husband a dirty look. "No one wants to hear from the peanut gallery, especially since Walker's doing me a favor. Stop busting his chops."

Nathan smothered a grin and did his best to appear mollified. Cassie turned her back on the two men. Walker did a little dance with hand signals that included Nathan crying after being scolded. His friend sent him a return gesture that wasn't kind. Juvenile, yes, but funny. Walker left his friend to pet Boone while he turned his focus back to Midnight.

The horse watched warily. Walker took a step toward Midnight. The metal joint in his knee complained, pain shooting up his thigh. Shoot. He must've injured it while lunging away from the horse. It'd taken three surgeries and a lot of physical therapy to put his body back together after a suicide bomber attacked a place of worship while he was on deployment. Still, Walker had been fortunate. Other members of his team, along with dozens of civilians, hadn't survived.

Shaking off the pain, he stepped forward again. Walker kept his movements confident and his tone calming. Horses were like dogs. They could sense fear and anxiety. Although Midnight had just tried to crack Walker's skull, he needed to approach the animal with gentle firmness. "It's okay, boy. I won't hurt you."

Midnight eyed him with distrust. Walker couldn't blame him. Some whips marks were fresh. Others were old. Very old. How long had this poor animal suffered at some horrible human's hand? Anger at the horse's mistreatment sparked through his veins, but Walker had enough military training to lock those emotions away. They wouldn't help him. Right now, Midnight needed control and calm.

Walker took another few steps toward the horse. "That's it, boy."

He kept talking to Midnight as he continued to approach. A Percheron, eighteen hands tall, the horse was an intimidating size, even as malnourished as he was. Patience and slow movements were essential. Walker had grown up around horses and had trained several, but none of them had been abused. It was a new experience. One he had to get right.

Midnight whinnied. He attempted to move away, but Walker shifted to block his escape. Then he crept closer. Keeping his voice low, he repeated reassuring words. Eventually, the horse allowed him to reach out a hand and take the lead rope hanging from the halter.

"Great job." Cassie stood in the center of the paddocks. "Now take him into the barn. Then you'll feed him immediately, so he associates the building with safety and food."

Walker nodded in acknowledgement of her instructions. To his relief, Midnight entered the barn and stall without a problem. Minutes later, he was happily munching on a pile of feed.

Walker dusted hay off his work gloves. "All right then. We're in business."

Cassie hugged him briefly, the kind of embrace a sister gave to a brother. The touch caused an unexpected swell of emotion inside Walker. Her kindness and love of horses reminded him so much of Lauren. His younger sister had been murdered almost a decade ago. It was an open wound, made worse because the killer had never been brought to justice. A fact Walker was determined to change.

He would never stop hunting Casanova. Not until the man was behind bars for his crimes.

"Thank you for doing this," Cassie said, pulling Walker from his thoughts. She stepped back. "I don't know how I can repay you."

"Think nothing of it." Walker's mouth twitched. "But if a batch of Bessie's chocolate chip oatmeal cookies arrived, I wouldn't be upset about it."

Cassie's aunt was famous for her baked goods and supplied them to the local coffee shop in town. Bessie's cookies couldn't be beat, in Walker's humble opinion. He'd devoured half a dozen all by himself at their last gathering. Of course, Walker would've housed Midnight completely for free, but being paid in cookies wasn't a bad bargain if he could get it.

Cassie winked. "You got it."

They stepped back into the waning sunshine. It would be dusk soon. Walker took a deep breath of the crisp air scented with grass, pine, and horses. Blue Star Ranch had been in his family for generations. Sprawling pastures stretched as far as the eye could see. White picket fences separated the barn from the main house and horses grazed freely within those confines. The cattle were kept farther back, rotated through separate areas of the property by ranch hands that stayed in the bunkhouse.

Walker tugged off a glove. "Why don't you and Nathan come up to the house for dinner? My parents would love to see you." He yanked at the other glove before tucking the pair in his back pocket. "Especially Dad. He's been a bear since breaking his leg last week and could use the company."

His father's horse had been spooked by a snake and thrown him. The doctors were confident he'd make a full recovery, but he was currently in a cast healing from a double fracture. Shane Montgomery wasn't one for sitting around. He'd attempted to go outside several times since coming home from the hospital. Walker's mom, Aileen, threatened to tie her husband to the couch daily.

Cassie dusted dirt from her top. "That sounds nice. Let me talk to Nathan and make sure he doesn't have something pressing..." Her brow crinkled. "Who is that?"

Walker's gaze shifted to the road just beyond the paddock. Nathan had one hand on the horse trailer, as if he'd been caught in the middle of closing it. He was talking to a dark-haired woman with her back to them. Something about her stature was familiar, but Walker couldn't place it. Then Nathan gestured toward Walker and Cassie. The woman turned.

Walker stumbled.

Cassie's hand shot out and grabbed his arm, steadying him. Her gaze swept across his face. "Are you okay? You look like you've seen a ghost." Her attention turned back to the woman. "Do you know her?"

He nodded in response to Cassie's question, but Walker's gaze was locked on his former high school sweetheart. His first love.

Hayley Barlow.

Memories slammed into him one after the other. Riding through the fields, walking through the halls of Knoxville High together, stolen kisses under a sky of stars. They'd had a sweet romance during senior year. And then, three months before graduation... the unthinkable happened.

Hayley left the high school library and found Walker's sister sitting on the curb. Lauren was waiting for Walker to pick her up after volleyball practice, but a flat tire had delayed him. Hayley kindly offered Lauren a ride home. Neither of the teenagers knew a killer was waiting in the back seat of Hayley's beat-up sedan. At gunpoint, Casanova ordered Hayley to drive to a remote location. What transpired next was something out of a horror film. Casanova shot Lauren and left her body in the woods like a pile of trash. Then he held Hayley for days until she escaped.

She came home alive. Lauren was buried in the cemetery.

And everything changed.

It was ten years, almost to the day, since Walker had last seen Hayley. She moved toward him on long strides full of confidence and purpose. Delicate cheekbones were offset by a full mouth and a high forehead. Her dark hair had once fallen in waves down her back. Now it was cut in a pixie style that suited her features. She could've passed for a model, except her gaze when it locked on him, was sharp. Pointed. Walker had seen such a look before on seasoned soldiers. On survivors of trauma. On cops.

Hayley was all three. The last Walker heard, she was a military police officer stationed at Fort Bragg. Her sudden appearance in Knoxville—on his ranch—was a shock.

Walker gathered his wits, murmured an excuse-me to Cassie, and set an intercept course for Hayley. She came to a sliding stop in front of him. It was unseasonably cold. Hayley was dressed for the weather in a wool coat and a scarf. Her lips were chapped.

"Hi, Walker."

Her gaze trailed over his face, and for a moment, he had the sense she was cataloging the differences time had made. Lines fanned out from the corners of his eyes, a faded scar earned in the desert half a world away on his first deployment marred his cheek, and stubble grew on his jaw line. Then warmth infused Hayley's expression. He was tempted to step forward and hug her in greeting, but the words she'd spoken during their last conversation played in his mind.

I'm sorry. I can't be around you. It's better this way.

Walker hooked his hands in the pockets of his jeans. "Hiya, Hails."

The nickname slipped out before he could catch it. A faint smile lifted the corners of Hayley's mouth, but a breath later, it was gone. "I'm sorry to drop by unexpectedly, but I need to ask. Has the Medina County Sheriff's Department talked to you?"

He blinked, caught completely off-guard by her question. "No." Walker stiffened as his pulse kicked into high gear. "Why?"

She muttered something under her breath. Then she met his gaze. "We need to talk. It's important."

THREE

She didn't want to be there.

Hayley was a living, breathing reminder of Lauren's murder. The last thing she wanted was to bring more pain to the Montgomery family. They didn't deserve it. But Casanova—and the sheriff's department—had left her no choice.

There was a woman in danger. And right now, no one was looking for her.

Hayley tightened her hand around the mug filled to the brim with fresh coffee. Dusk lengthened the shadows, creating a pattern across the tile floor in Walker's kitchen. His home was small but cozy. A combination of leather furnishings and worn wood designed to fit in with a simple country life. The kitchen had shaker cabinets and a pebbled countertop. No curtains, just shutters to block the view of the ranch at night. Thick trees surrounding the house provided a sense of privacy. The main house where his parents lived was within walking distance, as was the barn, but neither was visible from Hayley's vantage point.

Walker's dog, Boone, nudged her hand before sitting next to her chair. His soulful brown eyes stared up at her, pleading for attention.

She obliged by stroking his head. His fur was soft under her fingertips, his coat a beautiful pattern of brown, black, and white. "I never pictured you with a hound dog, Walker. You were always fond of Labradors."

"Still am, but Boone showed up on the ranch one day shortly after I got out of the Navy, looking bedraggled and hungry." Walker poured his own cup of coffee. The mug was black with the words Best Son scrolled across the front. A gift from his parents, no doubt. "I tried looking for Boone's owners, but no one claimed him. Now he's mine."

"Probably for the best." She scratched the dog behind his floppy ear. "Sounds like your previous owners didn't take good care of you."

Boone kissed her hand in response and then laid his head down on her leg. His eyes closed in bliss under her ministrations. Despite the awful reason for Hayley's arrival on the ranch, a smile formed on her lips. She'd always loved dogs. They were loyal and easy to understand. Nicer than most people, in her opinion.

"Last I heard, you were in the Army working as an MP." Walker leaned against the island. He'd shed his jacket and cowboy hat in the entryway. Time and age had added weight to his frame, all of it muscle, judging by the way the checked flannel shirt pulled tight across his broad chest. Worn jeans encased thighs the size of tree trunks. His hair was still a golden brown, but he sported a five o'clock shadow along the edge of his well-defined jaw. "Still employed by Uncle Sam?"

"Not anymore." Walker had followed her career? A tangle of pleasure and curiosity twirled together at the knowledge. Hayley smashed it down. Now wasn't the time to dwell on what that might mean. She lifted her right hand, the scars from the bullet visible along her skin. "Shot in the line of duty. Medical discharge."

He grunted and tapped his left foot against the tile. "Knee replacement. Ended my career with the SEALs."

A familiar attraction flared to life in Hayley's belly as their eyes met. His were the color of the ocean. A mix of blue and green, the colors so deep she wanted to lose herself in them. But there was an edge to Walker that hadn't been there before. A current riding just below the surface of his calm expression that hinted of secrets and dark shadows. Regret. Pain. All of it tangled together and difficult to unknot.

The fun-loving teenager she'd once known was gone. The death of his sister and his time as a SEAL had transformed him. Hayley could relate. Age provided wisdom. It also left scars.

She stole a glance at his left hand. No wedding ring. The decor of his home suggested he was a bachelor, but Walker could have a girl-friend. Or a fiancée. A sinking feeling nestled in the pit of her stomach at the thought. Hayley tightened her hand around the coffee mug. It shouldn't matter. She wasn't here to connect with an old boyfriend.

"Where are you living now?" Walker asked, cutting into her thoughts.

"In North Carolina. My discharge was a few months ago and I'm trying to decide my next career move." She shifted in the chair. "Policing isn't an option for me anymore, but it's the only thing I ever wanted to do."

Her injury prevented her from being accurate enough with a handgun to pass the firearm exam. She was still better than the average person, and practice had improved things, but a career in law enforcement was impossible.

Walker tilted his head. "You could become a PI. I have a friend from the SEALs who started his own business. Travis is successful with it."

"It's something to consider. I don't know." Hayley took a drink of her coffee. The warm liquid coursed down her throat. "Suddenly being out of the military has been jarring. Uncle Sam decided where I lived and managed my career path. It's strange to think I could go anywhere, do anything."

"Understandable. If I didn't have the ranch, I'd be lost."

"I'd forgotten how beautiful it is here." Hayley's gaze drifted to the window and the view beyond. The natural beauty stirred a calm in her that couldn't be replicated in the city or suburbs. "How are your parents?"

Hayley hadn't gone to the main house when she arrived on the ranch, for good reason. Her presence could upset the older couple. A ranch hand repairing the front gate was kind enough to direct Hayley to the barn where Walker was.

"They're fine. Mom's still active in the church; Dad's busy running this place. They've been approved to become foster parents." His lips curved into a smile. "A tactic to soothe the urge for grandkids, I imagine."

Curiosity got the better of her. "You're not married?"

"Nope. Not even dating, much to Mom's dismay." Walker lightly arched his brows. "You?"

Her cheeks flushed. "No."

She'd tried to date here and there over the years. Unsuccessfully. Hayley was incredibly slow to trust. A difficult childhood, coupled with the traumatic experience of being held captive, had created a protective wall around her emotions. Therapy had helped with her PTSD. It'd also opened her up to the possibility of falling in love. But none of the men she dated were patient enough to get past her initial hesitancy.

Not that she could blame them. Hayley rarely discussed her drug-addicted mother and being kidnapped by Casanova. It wasn't the type of conversation to have on a first date. Or a second one. None of the men she'd dated understood the trauma she'd been through.

And now Casanova was back.

A tremble skittered across her skin. Hayley kept stroking Boone's head. The dog sighed, the air puffing across her legs, as an awkward hush fell in the kitchen. Walker must've sensed the shift in her thoughts, because he stayed quiet, letting her work through them. He'd always been intuitive that way.

Hayley chewed on the inside of her lower lip. This conversation wouldn't be easy. "My mom died a few days ago. That's why I'm in town."

She heard his sharp intake of breath. Then a chair scraped against the floor. Walker sat across from her. "I'm sorry, Hails. I didn't know..."

"There's no way you could have."

She'd been the one to cut contact with Walker. It seemed a natural step after everything that'd transpired, but Hayley had cried for months afterward. A childhood of neglect had created an unhealthy distrust in almost everyone. Walker had been one of the few to slip past her walls. He'd shown her gentleness and a glimpse of normalcy. Their friendship—even more valuable than the romance— was the thing she'd mourned most.

The weight of Boone's head still rested against Hayley's leg. She reached down to stroke his fur again, letting the repeated motion soothe her. "Last night, I arrived home after the funeral to discover someone had been in my mother's house."

Hayley quickly described the creepy call from Casanova. Walker remained silent the entire time, but his expression turned stone hard. Then she pulled out her cell phone and tapped on the screen. "When I opened the envelope, there were two things inside. A letter and a bracelet."

She turned the device toward Walker, the letter enlarged enough to be legible. It was typewritten on computer paper. The original had been taken into evidence, but before calling the sheriff's department, Hayley had photographed everything.

Walker read aloud. "My sweetheart, you were clever enough to escape from me. Let's find out if you're smart enough to stop a murder. Locate the owner of this bracelet before time runs out. Don't call the police, or I'll kill her and find someone new to play the game.

Signed, Casanova."

Hayley touched the screen. "There's a postscript."

"Tell Walker hi for me."

A muscle in his jaw worked and his fingers turned white against the cell phone. Hayley feared for a moment he would break it. She gently tugged it from his hand and tapped on the next photograph before turning it to face him. "Do you recognize this bracelet?"

He studied the twist of gold and pearls. Anna was etched into a decorative plate in the center. Hayley had been up most of the night doing internet searches, attempting to figure out who the designer was, but to no avail. She held her breath, watching the emotions flicker across Walker's expression. Recognition wasn't one of them.

He blew out a breath. "I've never seen that piece of jewelry before in my life."

Disappointment crushed her. Who was Anna? How could Hayley find her if she didn't know where to look?

"I take it you reported the incident to the sheriff's department," Walker said, taking the phone from her hand and studying the bracelet again before returning to the letter.

Hayley nodded. Casanova had instructed her not to, but she was a former law enforcement officer. The break-in, the letter, and the threat required a formal investigation. "The detective who questioned me didn't seem to take it seriously. He suggested it was someone's idea of a practical joke."

Heat flooded her cheeks as anger spiked her blood pressure. She'd had a few choice words for Detective Jenkins, which hadn't endeared him to her cause, but nothing made Hayley madder than a law enforcement officer not doing his job. She hadn't expected him to believe Casanova had come back after ten years, but there was urgency in the matter. The threats were specific. Creepy. Elaborate.

And a woman's life was potentially on the line.

"A practical joke?" Walker reared back. "Seriously?"

"The Casanova case has been spun into something of a myth in the county." No one wanted to believe someone capable of kidnapping and murder lived in their small community. "Detective Jenkins suggested teenagers likely uncovered my connection to the case and designed a scheme to frighten me. He promised to contact you about the bracelet."

Unfortunately, Hayley had been left with a bad feeling that Detective Jenkins wouldn't follow through on his word. Which is why she'd phoned him several times throughout the day. He never returned her call. Frustrated and desperate, Hayley had driven to Blue Star Ranch. "Are you sure the bracelet isn't familiar? I'd hoped, since Casanova mentioned you specifically, that you'd know who the owner was and could provide a last name."

Walker's expression was grim. "I don't think Casanova mentioned me in the letter because I could identify the bracelet."

"Then why did he? Because of Lauren?"

"Not exactly." He pushed away from the table and waved for her to stand. "Come on. There's something you need to see."

Hayley gently pushed Boone off her knee and followed Walker out of the kitchen. The pup trailed behind them to the hallway. His nails clicked against the wood flooring.

Walker made an abrupt left into what was supposed to be a spare bedroom, but had been converted into an office. A wide oak desk was positioned in front of a picture window. Bookshelves lined one wall. On the opposite side was the biggest corkboard Hayley had ever seen. A giant map of the state was pinned to it, along with photographs, documents, and dates.

Lauren's picture from the high school yearbook was at the top of the board. Her hair was streaked blonde from the sun, her smile crooked, a dimple in her left cheek flashing. Hayley's picture was right next to Lauren's. Her expression was more serious. Guarded. The date of their kidnapping was underneath. A red string had been tied around the pin and stretched to the map. The location of Knoxville High School was marked.

Understanding slammed into Hayley all at once. She'd used a similar setup when investigating cases. "This is a murder board."

"Yes." Walker planted his hands on his hips. "I've been investigating my sister's case for the last two years. Unlike the police, I never believed Casanova was dead. I'm determined to find him." His gaze swept across the board, locking on the image of his little sister. Lauren had only been eleven months younger than Walker. They'd been very close. "I suspect Casanova is aware of my investigation."

"Which is why he singled you out in the letter." Hayley's mind whirled as she scanned the murder board. Several photographs of dark-haired women were neatly lined up on the left-hand side. Each picture had a corresponding string that stretched to the map. A sick feeling of dread balled in her stomach. She pointed to the images. "Who are they?"

"Missing women." Walker's voice was low. Haunted. She sensed hesitation, and then he continued, "I suspect Casanova continued killing after your escape. A man like that doesn't just stop or disappear."

She slammed her eyes shut, momentarily blocking out the world. Her stomach cramped. Bile rose in the back of Hayley's throat. Some part of her, way deep down, had suspected the same. But she hadn't wanted to acknowledge it. She didn't want to now.

Please, God, I want Detective Jenkins to be right. This is just some kids playing a very nasty prank. I can't do this.

The prayer was instinctive, and normally calming, but this time, it had little effect. Hayley snapped open her eyes. "Thomas Daniels committed suicide two years after I escaped from Casanova. The police chief of Knoxville assured me that Thomas was Casanova. He was so certain..."

Hayley had been held in a shed on Thomas's land. After her escape, Casanova burned the structure to the ground. That left the police with little physical evidence. They questioned Thomas several times, but he denied any involvement in Hayley's kidnapping or in

Lauren's murder. His property was vast, the location of the shed in an area that hadn't been used in over twenty years. It was overgrown and unfenced. Anyone could've snuck on and off without the Daniels's knowing.

"Chief Walters was corrupt," Walker said. "It was discovered that he manipulated cases. His conclusions can't be relied on."

She hugged herself. "And the current chief?"

"Sam Garcia is a good man and an excellent law enforcement officer, but his jurisdiction is limited to the city of Knoxville." Walker stepped forward and used his finger to circle areas the missing women had disappeared from. "As you can see, most are beyond the town limits. Chief Garcia can't investigate their disappearances."

No, he couldn't. The cases stretched across multiple counties, which meant several law enforcement departments would be involved. A jurisdictional nightmare. Hayley stepped closer to the photographs and then the map. She forced her brain to snap into work mode. "How do you know these women are Casanova's victims?"

"I don't. At least, not conclusively. They're single brunettes ranging in ages from 25 to 40. All of them have disappeared from public places, either with their vehicle—suggesting a carjacking—or while walking on the street. None of them have been seen again. Their credit cards haven't been used, nor have their bank accounts been accessed. Their cell phones are turned off and tossed near the place of their abductions." He was quiet for the long moment. "And they all look like you."

She automatically wanted to take a step back, as if recoiling from his words, but forced herself to stand strong. Her gaze once again swung to the photographs lined on the corkboard. Walker was right. The women all resembled her.

None of the information Walker provided was enough to conclusively determine the cases were linked, but it was worth checking into. "Have you told anyone in law enforcement about this?"

"My cousin Ryker is with the Texas Rangers. He's been helping me, but even he has to abide by the rules. Texas Rangers have to be invited onto a case."

Hayley rocked back on her heels. Today was full of surprises. "Ryker's a Texas Ranger?" Walker's cousin had been a bull-riding wild child the last time she saw him. "Seriously?"

Walker's mouth twitched. "He's changed."

"I guess we all have."

Including Casanova. If Walker was correct, the criminal hadn't been simply hiding out for the last ten years. He'd been practicing, honing his horrific skills, until he was a proficient serial killer. A shudder rippled down Hayley's spine. She pulled up the letter on her phone and read it again, this time with her investigative cap on. She'd worked numerous murders during her time in law enforcement.

"He's pitting us against each other." She tapped an index finger against her phone. "It's some kind of twisted competition." Unease settled like a weight across her shoulders. Hayley flipped to the photograph of the bracelet. Without a doubt, she believed Casanova had selected his next victim. Fresh urgency coursed through her veins. "I need to find this woman before he makes good on his promise."

Walker was quiet for a long moment. "You don't recognize the bracelet and neither do I. Let's assume that Casanova has provided a solid clue. There has to be some way of identifying her. Is he counting on the sheriff's department doing the legwork?"

"I doubt it. He specifically instructed me *not* to call the police. No, this woman has to be someone we know or someone we can identify..." Hayley shook her head in frustration.

Walker ran a hand over his stubble. "What about checking with the Knoxville Police Department? You and Lauren were kidnapped from their jurisdiction. Maybe Casanova is hunting in familiar grounds."

"It's worth a shot."

At this point, Hayley would do anything to find Anna. *Please, God. Help me.*

FOUR

The Knoxville Police Department was a squat, red-brick building with large windows overlooking Main Street. There was a small reception area that led to a squad room. Several hallways arched toward the rear of the building, presumably leading to interview rooms and the jail. The floor was scuffed and worn, as was the furniture, and the scent of burnt coffee permeated every inch.

Hayley instantly felt at home.

There was an energy to a well-run law enforcement department. It couldn't be faked or forced, but when it existed, it was obvious. And in Hayley's experience, the tone was always set by the leader. Within moments of meeting Chief Sam Garcia, she understood why Walker trusted him. The chief exuded confidence and self-assurance, but wasn't arrogant. His brown hair was peppered with gray and the faint shadows under his eyes spoke of long hours. As Hayley explained Casanova's threat, the chief carefully took notes on a legal pad. He interrupted only to ask clarifying questions. Concern formed a furrow in his brow, and when Hayley was done, he set his pen down.

"No one has been reported missing in the last several days." He picked up Hayley's phone from the desk and enlarged the photograph of the bracelet with two fingers. "However, my officers can pull anyone by the name of Anna from our town registry and we can start knocking on doors. I'll need a copy of this photograph along with the one of the letter."

Hayley breathed out a sigh of relief. "Of course, whatever you need." She took her phone from him and quickly typed in his email address to send the photos.

"Did the sheriff's department fingerprint your mother's home?"

She nodded, clicking the side button on her phone to lock the screen. "I insisted on it. They didn't get any decent prints off the items Casanova touched, which isn't surprising. He's smart enough to have used gloves."

The chief grunted in agreement. "Before coming to Knoxville, I spent several years with the FBI and occasionally worked with MPs when a case overlapped in jurisdiction. The Army trains well."

"They do."

"Although you've left the military, I still consider you a member of the law enforcement community, so I'll shoot straight with you. The Medina County Sheriff's Department is short-staffed and over-worked. Detective Jenkins is a solid investigator, but his boss—the sheriff—is selective about where man hours are spent."

Hayley understood exactly where the chief was going. "He won't take a threatening letter seriously."

"Not without more evidence. I will contact the sheriff personally and express my concern, but of course, I have no control over whether he'll investigate further." Chief Garcia folded his hands across his desk. "To be honest, this could be as Detective Jenkins said. Some kids playing a practical joke."

Her gaze narrowed. "Is that what you think?"

"I don't know. There's not much evidence to go on." The chief's mouth flattened into a thin line. "But I won't lie. I'm concerned about the prospect of Casanova's return. If he's playing some kind of game, then he's working off a plan. I wasn't a part of the Knoxville Police Department when you were kidnapped, but after becoming chief, I read the case file. Casanova was organized. Precise. Cruel. I don't want someone like that roaming our streets."

Hayley agreed. "Why haven't you had Lauren's murder re-investigated then?"

"The sheriff's department isn't the only one short-staffed and overworked. I've put in a request with the city to hire more investigators, so we can form a cold case division, but the budget hasn't been allocated yet. Lauren's murder isn't the only one I'd like solved." Chief Garcia suddenly looked weary. "The town's population has exploded over the last several years, and unfortunately, so has the crime rate. It's been difficult to keep up with current cases."

"I understand." Budgets and staffing were a problem everywhere. So far, Chief Garcia had taken her concerns seriously, and she was grateful. Hayley rose. "I appreciate everything you're doing to locate Anna."

Chief Garcia also stood. "One more thing. I don't mean to step out of bounds, but Anna isn't the only person I'm concerned about." He leveled a piercing gaze on Hayley. "Casanova broke into your mother's home, called your cell, and left a threatening note. I have the deepest respect for your military service, but everyone could benefit from having someone watch their back."

He gestured toward the glass wall overlooking the squad room. Walker was deep in conversation with an officer. Both men wore grave expressions, and Hayley had the impression they were discussing the case.

"Walker is part of a group I fondly call the Special Forces," Chief Garcia continued. "All of them are veterans like yourself who were injured in the line of duty. In recent years, they've assisted others in town who needed help." He rested his hands on his duty belt and it creaked. "If I know Walker, he'll offer to protect you. I strongly recommend you accept."

Hayley wasn't sure what to think about that. She was used to taking care of herself, but the chief was right. Every good law enforcement officer—not to mention soldier—knew it was valuable to have a trusted person watching your six.

And maybe Walker needed her as much as she needed him. Casanova had mentioned the former SEAL specifically in his letter. It worried Hayley. "Are you aware that Walker has been investigating his sister's murder case?"

"I am. He's not doing anything illegal and any information he uncovers is shared with my department. Unfortunately, it hasn't yielded any new suspects."

"Thomas Daniels had a son. Walker and I went to high school with him. Bobby Ray. Where is he now?"

"Prison. Or was until recently. Bobby Ray was released two weeks ago and is currently on parole." Chief Garcia's brow arched. "I'll have a deputy stop by and see where Bobby Ray was during the time of the break-in at your mom's."

Hayley smiled. "Appreciate it, Chief. And thank you for the advice."

She shook the older man's hand before exiting his office. Walker was still in deep conversation with the officer in the squad room. Both men fell silent when she approached. It irked her, although it shouldn't have. Their body language indicated the men were good friends. They could've been discussing something personal.

Walker offered Hayley a smile and gestured to the auburn-haired man next to him. "Hayley, I'd like you to meet my friend, Tucker Colburn. He's a former Army Ranger turned police officer."

"Nice to meet you, ma'am." Tucker shook Hayley's hand. His grip was firm, but not bruising, and his gaze direct. Crisp lines showed someone had pressed his uniform with care. He gave off a competent and no nonsense impression. A wedding ring flashed on his left hand, and behind him on the desk was a photo of Tucker with a curly-haired woman in glasses. The couple looked incredibly happy standing on a mountaintop in hiking gear with two dogs.

"You can call me Hayley." She dropped his hand, her lips curling into a smile. "Walker's friend and a former Army Ranger. That would make you a member of the Special Forces, I take it."

Tucker chuckled. "Guilty." His expression grew serious. "I understand the sheriff's department didn't take your concerns about the break-in and Casanova's threat seriously. Please know that won't be the case with us. We'll do everything we can to look into the matter."

His tone was matter-of-fact. Hayley immediately liked him, which was a rare occurrence for her. She was generally guarded when meeting new people. "Thank you." She gestured to the photograph on Tucker's desk. "Is that your wife? She's beautiful."

He beamed. "Yes, that's Leah. She runs the Knoxville Animal Shelter. If you stay in town long enough, I'm sure you'll meet her." Tucker's grin widened. "A word of warning. She'll convince you to adopt a stray dog or cat. Those mutts in the picture with us are rescues. Leah never met an animal she didn't instantly fall in love with."

Hayley got the sense she would like Leah just as much as she did Tucker. "I hope to get the chance to meet her."

Tucker nodded. "We'll make it happen. I'm sure all the wives will want to meet you." He smacked Walker on the chest. "This lump is the last man standing. The only one in the group who isn't married. He practically repels women with his ugly face."

Walker pushed back. "Have you looked in a mirror lately? Leah manages somehow."

"Yes, but I don't have horrible taste in pie." Tucker wagged his eyebrows in Hayley's direction before screwing up his nose like he'd smelled something nasty. "Lemon meringue is an abomination against humanity. This dude eats it at least once a week."

Hayley laughed. She couldn't stand lemon meringue either, but

Tucker was right. Walker had always loved it. "He's got you there, Montgomery."

"Don't." Walker pointed a finger at her. "You have to be on my side. I've been your friend since high school. You just met this fool."

She pressed her lips together to smother another laugh and then nodded in mock seriousness. "You're right."

"It's okay, Hayley." Tucker winked. "You and I know the truth."

Walker gave his friend another friendly push. Chief Garcia called Tucker's name and waved to indicate the officer should come into his office. Tucker immediately snapped into professional mode. He clapped Walker on the back and gave a nod to Hayley before hurrying across the squad room.

The two men disappeared into the chief's office.

Hayley turned to Walker. "I like him. Are the rest of the guys in your friend group as nice?"

"Yep. Every one of them has helped me at one time or another. It's hard to adjust to civilian life after being in the military. Having friends who understand the difficulties and can provide support makes all the difference." They headed for the exit, and Walker's expression grew serious. "What happened with the chief?"

Hayley gave him a rundown of the conversation. As she talked, the muscles in her shoulders loosened. Chief Garcia's competence was a balm to her stress and worries. Someone in an official capacity was taking her seriously and that meant the chances of finding Anna increased incrementally. "I asked the chief about Bobby Ray, Thomas's son. Apparently, he was released from prison recently. It's possible Thomas was Casanova, as the previous chief believed, and his son has taken over the persona. Or maybe Bobby Ray is Casanova."

"I never liked Bobby Ray, but I find it difficult to believe he has the brains to pull something like this off." Walker tucked his hands into the pocket of his jacket. "He's more of a petty criminal. His rap sheet consists of simple burglary and drug possession."

Hayley pictured the bulky teen she once knew. Bobby Ray was a boxer, even back in high school, with a meaty right hook and a mean streak to match. "I wouldn't be so quick to write him off. Bobby Ray was manipulative. He didn't get into much trouble in high school, but I know he was into a lot of things." Bitterness coated her voice. "He sold my mom drugs. Others too."

Walker grunted. "I'm not defending him—the man is a criminal—but selling drugs and murder are two different things."

"I know." She zipped up her jacket to ward against the frigid night air. "You were right to suggest we come here. Chief Garcia is taking the case seriously. Still, it's frustrating. I can't believe Casanova would make it so hard to identify the woman. There's something I'm missing."

"I wouldn't assume that he's playing fair." Walker came to a stop next to his truck and turned to face her. The lighting in the parking lot was dim, but there was understanding and sympathy etched along the powerful lines of his features. "You've done everything you can."

"Doesn't make this any easier." Hayley shoved her hands in her pockets. She licked her chapped lips, uncertain about whether to speak her inner most thoughts out loud. But Walker would understand. Probably the only one who could. "It's tearing me up inside... imagining him holding someone captive."

"Hails."

Just one word, but the compassion in his voice brought tears to her eyes. Walker reached for her, but she stepped back, afraid that if he touched her, the last shred of her composure would shatter.

He dropped his hand immediately, taking a big step back. "Sorry, I don't want to make you uncomfortable."

"No, it's not you." Hayley sucked in a breath to steady her emotions. "It's been a long day, and I didn't sleep much last night." Or the night before. If she was being honest, she hadn't slept well since setting foot back in Knoxville. Being here drudged up memories, and her mother's funeral had been more taxing than she'd anticipated. "I'm tired."

"Then let's get on the road." Walker reached for the door handle of the passenger side of his truck.

A red dot danced across the edge of his jacket.

"Sniper!" Hayley's heart jumped into her throat. She lunged toward Walker, slamming her shoulder into his waist. Glass shattered as they tumbled to the ground in a tangle of limbs. She felt, rather than heard, the air whoosh from Walker's lungs. Still, his arms came around her protectively as bullets slammed into the truck.

More glass rained down. Followed by even more bullets. Walker pushed Hayley under the truck, but there was no safe place to go.

They were pinned down.

FIVE

Walker pushed Hayley deeper under the truck, desperate to keep her safe from the sniper shooting at them. Glass pebbles rained down on his head and coat. Pain arched along his scalp and the warm trickle of blood followed. He ignored it. The shooter was across the street, on the roof of the courthouse. He pulled his weapon, but the handgun was no match for a rifle.

Hayley tugged on his arm. "Get under the truck."

He did as she instructed, wrapping his body protectively around hers. Metal pinged as bullets collided with the vehicle. Walker's heart thundered in his chest and his mind shot back to the desert. Sand against his skin and the scent of blood. Screams from the injured.

He sucked in a breath and forced the images away. Consciously focused on the cold air flooding his lungs, the bits of gravel poking his skin through the fabric of his jeans, and Hayley's presence in his arms. The scent of her perfume filled his nostrils. Something tropical that reminded him of warm beaches and sunshine. It was familiar and twisted his heart in painful ways.

He'd missed her. Unexpected grief swelled, rocketing his emotions into an unwanted place. Lauren's murder had shaken Walker to his core, shattering the innocence and hopefulness he'd carried even in his teenage years. Losing Hayley had added salt to the wound. She'd been his best friend. The months following Lauren's funeral were spent holding himself together by sheer strength of will. Walker's parents had been grief-stricken, too caught up in their own pain to worry about his.

It didn't help that he left home for the Navy shortly after graduation. He poured himself into his military career. Protecting innocents and serving his country had given him purpose but did little to ease his suffering. The SEALs taught him to bury those emotions. Focus on the mission and get the job done. But it didn't erase the past. It simply went into a box Walker kept tightly closed. But every once in a while... it opened just enough for some emotion to leak out.

Like now.

Walker battled against the feelings threatening to overwhelm him, locking them away as he slipped into soldier mode. Hayley needed his protection. He couldn't keep her safe if he was lost in the past.

Silence fell. It was extremely loud in the wake of the gunshots.

"Is he shifting positions for another attempt?" Hayley whispered. "Or is he escaping?"

"There's no way to know from this vantage point. Stay here. I'll assess the situation." Walker started to shift out from underneath the truck, but Hayley grabbed his arm, halting his movements.

"Don't. He was aiming for you."

Before Walker could respond, the door to the police department opened. Tucker appeared in tactical gear, a shield held in one hand to protect him from the sniper's bullets. Several more officers poured from the building. Sirens blared as emergency vehicles—police officers that'd been on patrol along with sheriff's deputies—responded to the incident. Soon the street was flooded with law enforcement.

"Walker, you hit?" Tucker appeared next to the vehicle.

"No, we're okay." He scooted out from under the truck but stayed in a crouch. The sniper could be anywhere. Then he offered a hand to Hayley as she also slipped out.

Tucker handed them protective vests, and they slipped them on before running across the parking lot. Walker almost expected more shots to be fired, but nothing happened. They burst into the police department and then Tucker hustled them into an interview room. A stainless-steel table was bolted to the floor, surrounded by plastic chairs. Cameras were discreetly hung from the ceiling. The room had no windows.

Relief took the edge off the adrenaline coursing through Walker's veins. He shoved his handgun back into its holster. His gaze swept across Hayley. Oil marks smudged her jeans and the strands of her hair were mussed, but she was in one piece. "Are you hurt?"

"No, but you are." Concern darkened her brown eyes until they were almost the same shade of black as her hair. She lifted a slender hand and pointed to his head. "You're bleeding. Tucker, we need a first aid kit."

"I'm fine." Walker touched the scrape in his hairline. The wound barely hurt, but his hand came away coated with blood. "It's just a scratch."

Tucker ignored him, dipping out of the room. Moments later, he returned with a first aid kit, which he handed to Hayley. "Once things are secure, I'll send a paramedic to look at him." Tucker caught the dirty look Walker sent him and scowled. "Don't be a pain. Logan's working tonight. He'll ride my tail for weeks if I don't let him examine you."

Walker opened his mouth to launch a retort, but Tucker was already gone. The door closed behind him with a faint click.

Hayley pulled out a chair. "Sit. Let me see how bad it is."

He didn't want to be babied. Walker's muscles ached to exit the interview room and hunt down the sniper on his own. But that would mean leaving Hayley unprotected, not to mention impeding law enforcement. He hated being on the sidelines.

"Maybe you should be the one to sit." Walker frowned. "You look pale."

Her mouth twitched with amusement as she snagged his wrist and shoved him into a chair. "I'm not the one bleeding all over my jacket. You SEAL boys are all the same. Thick headed to the point of entering the Neanderthal zone."

"Exactly how many Navy SEALs have you worked with. You were in the Army."

He said Army like it was a dirty word. Walker genuinely respected every military branch, but it was well known there was a healthy competition between them. As he'd hoped, Walker's comment brought another smile to Hayley's face. Her cheeks were gaining some color back.

She ripped open a disinfectant cloth and used it to clean her hands. "Who's Logan? Another member of the Special Forces?"

"Yep. Logan was a medic in the Air Force. Now he works for the Knoxville EMS."

"What exactly did you guys do to earn that nickname from the chief?" Hayley opened a package of gauze and pressed it to the cut. The wound was near Walker's ear. "Hold this for me."

He did as she asked. Walker realized Hayley was making small talk to distract from the chaos happening beyond the interview room. Her fingers trembled as she organized the supplies needed to doctor his wound, although there was no tension in her muscles or worry in her expression. She was good at that. Compartmentalizing. Always had been. The side-effects of a childhood marked by negligence and sorrow.

Walker gave her a condensed version of the cases he and his friends had become embroiled in over the years. She peppered him with questions here and there, but mostly Hayley listened. Her touch against his skin was gentle. A cute furrow formed between her brows as she cleaned the wound. Over and over again, Walker was distracted by her.

Time had only enhanced Hayley's beauty. It'd smoothed away the soft lines of youth, leaving her exquisite features more defined. Bangs fluttered across her forehead, drawing attention to wide-set eyes the color of fall—a rich brown with hints of gold and auburn. The scars on her right hand were raw, angry red streaks that would fade eventually. As she reached up to put antiseptic on his wound, her shirtsleeve rode up, revealing a tattoo on the inside of her wrist.

Before Walker could consciously think about it, he gently captured her hand and turned it to see the writing embedded in her skin. His breath caught. "Hebrews 11:1."

"Lauren's favorite Bible verse." Hayley's voice was low, barely above a whisper. "Now faith is confidence in what we hope for and assurance in what we do not see."

Something twisted hard inside Walker, perilously close to bringing him to tears. Hayley hadn't been a believer before they started dating in high school. His family invited her to church. Then Lauren invited Hayley to her Bible study group. Her faith had grown from there.

He traced his fingers over the tattoo. Hayley's skin was silky, and her breath hitched. Walker lifted his gaze to meet hers. "Did you get this to remember Lauren?"

"Yes. And as a reminder to myself. When I was locked in the shed, this verse got me through."

He didn't know what to say. Walker's own faith had taken a stumble since Lauren's death. He still prayed, still believed, but God felt far away. There was a broken place inside Walker that couldn't be repaired. The SEALs hadn't done it. Coming home hadn't either. Maybe getting justice for Lauren would... Perhaps then, he would feel the peace he longed for.

The door opened, breaking the moment. Hayley tugged her hand away from Walker as Tucker walked into the room. His expression was tight, his lips flattened into a firm line. "The sniper got away. We've got men canvassing, but I'm not holding my breath."

Walker mentally said a few choice words. He glanced at Hayley, but her expression was blank. Whatever she was thinking was hidden behind a careful mask.

"Stay here," Tucker continued. "Someone will come and take your statements soon."

He disappeared again.

Hayley snapped the first aid kit closed. "You should be okay. I don't think the cut needs stitches, but Logan will tell you for sure."

Walker didn't give a fig about his wound. They had bigger problems at the moment. "I want you to come and stay on my ranch tonight. Returning to your mom's house isn't a good idea, given the circumstances."

She shook her head. "Assuming the sniper was Casanova, he wasn't aiming for me. He was gunning for you. He tried to shoot you in front of me, just like..."

Walker didn't need her to finish the statement. He knew exactly what Hayley couldn't say.

Just like with Lauren.

A fresh wave of anger coursed through Walker's veins. He'd already figured out Casanova's motives, but it was painful to hear the faint tremble in Hayley's voice. She didn't deserve this. Not any of it. But now that things were set in motion, Hayley wouldn't back off. She'd go to the ends of the earth to find Casanova. It terrified Walker to think of Hayley hunting the killer by herself.

"Casanova is coming for me no matter what you do. Isn't it better if we work together to find him?" He sent her a charming smile. "That way you can watch my back like you did tonight. You would've made an awesome linebacker, Hails."

She snorted. "Nice try, Montgomery, but compliments won't get you anywhere."

"Then logic should. You know I'm right."

She was quiet for a long moment and then turned away from him. Hayley walked to the door. Through the small plexiglass window, controlled chaos reigned in the squad room. She hugged herself. "I appreciate the offer, Walker. Truly I do, but how are your parents going to feel if I stay on the ranch?"

His parents? They'd be furious if he left Hayley unprotected. She'd spent so much time at his house as a teen, his parents had practically considered her one of their own.

Walker stared in disbelief at the sharp line of her back. Why on earth would Hayley think his parents...

Oh, heavens. Like a bolt of lightning, understanding shot through him. "Hayley, no." In three strides, he crossed the room to her. Walker gently laid his hands on her shoulder and turned her body until she faced him. The pain in her eyes nearly stole his breath. "None of us, my parents included, blame you for Lauren's death. None of us. Do you hear me?"

Tears welled along her lashes. "I tried to save her."

"I know you did." Walker had read the statement Hayley gave to the police after being rescued. Lauren had frozen with fear when they were carjacked. Hayley had tried several times, in different ways, to help the younger teen escape. It was impossible. Lauren's response to terror had always been to freeze. There was nothing Hayley could have done.

Walker pulled her into his arms. Hayley's body shook with the force of her silent sobs. It broke his heart in two. "You're not to blame, Hails. You never were."

There was only one person responsible for Lauren's death.

Casanova.

And now, ten years later, he'd returned to finish what he'd started. As a SEAL, Walker was used to taking the fight to the enemy if need be, but now... he feared it might cost him more than he was willing to lose.

SIX

Walker breathed a sigh of relief as the truck's tires bounced over the cattle guard at the entrance of Blue Star Ranch. Exhaustion tugged at his muscles and the wound along his scalp was pounding. He needed pain medication. Hayley probably could use some too. She'd slammed into him pretty hard outside the police station.

Her quick actions had likely saved his life.

The sniper had damaged his vehicle, and it would need repairs. Luckily, there was a spare pickup on the farm. A couple of ranch hands dropped it off at the station while Walker and Hayley were giving their statements. The vehicle was dusty from hauling hay, the old dashboard cracked from sun damage, but underneath the hood, the engine purred like a kitten. It wasn't pretty, but the truck was more than serviceable.

Walker glanced in the rearview mirror to ensure the gate closed properly. His security system wasn't top-of-the-line, but everyone who entered the property needed a fob or had to ask for permission at the ranch entrance. Cameras were strategically placed at various locations. It was possible for someone to sneak onto the property, but no one could get close to the houses without Walker receiving an alert on his phone. Additionally, two of his friends—Jason and Kyle—would keep watch overnight.

Hayley was safe.

She sat quietly in the passenger seat next to him, staring at the scenery beyond the window as Walker followed the well-lit drive to the main house. Motion detection lights flipped on, illuminating the porch and yard. Boone came racing around the corner. His ears flapped as he barked up a storm and then let out a howl that could wake the dead.

Kyle and Jason followed Boone. Connor, a former military bomb-detection dog, trotted at Jason's side. The two had deployed together and been scarred by the same IED.

Walker exited the truck, the frosty night air embracing him as he lifted a hand in greeting to his friends before patting Boone on the head. "It's just me, you crazy mutt."

Boone wiggled with excitement, his tail whipping back and forth. The passenger-side door of the truck opened, and the dog abandoned Walker to greet Hayley. The sound of her lilting voice as she talked to Boone drifted on the breeze. Then she rounded the truck as Walker retrieved her suitcase from the rear seat of the cab. Before coming to the ranch, they'd stopped by her mom's house.

Hayley jerked her chin toward Jason and Kyle. "Two more of the Special Forces, I take it?"

He chuckled. "Yep. Jason is a former Marine and Kyle worked as a security specialist. Let me introduce you."

Walker hefted Hayley's laptop bag over his shoulder and set an intercept course for his friends. Hayley fell into step beside him, Boone following along at her heel. The mutt kept jumping up to lick her hand. Then he raced ahead to tackle Connor. The German shepherd ignored him, keeping pace with Jason, but Walker could've sworn there was an exacerbated look on his furry face.

"Boone." Walker snapped his fingers. "Heel."

The hound instantly obeyed. Boone might be troublesome and energetic, but he was trained.

The men greeted each other with handshakes and brotherly hugs. Then Walker introduced them to Hayley. They made small talk for a few minutes about their former military service. Connor lay down in the grass and Boone pranced around, as if begging the older dog to play.

Jason chuckled. The scar along the right side of his face shifted with the movement. "Boone is like an annoying baby brother to Connor. It'll be interesting to see how he reacts once Addison has the baby." He glanced at Hayley. "Addison's my wife. We're expecting our first child this spring."

"Congratulations." Hayley's smile was warm and genuine. "Well, I've just met Connor, but he's very patient with Boone, so I don't think you have anything to worry about."

Neither did Walker. He'd seen how protective Connor was with Addison and imagined the dog would be exactly the same with the baby. But that raised a fresh worry. When his friends offered to help protect Hayley, Walker had readily accepted but hadn't considered the impact it would have on their family lives.

Jason's wife was pregnant. Kyle had a toddler at home. All the members of the Special Forces were married, except Walker, and each of them had obligations to family and loved ones. Walker was a fool for not considering that earlier. He tightened his hold on Hayley's suitcase. "You know, Jason, if you need to be with Addison, there's no hard feelings. Kyle, same for you. I know you guys have responsibilities—"

"Let me stop you right there." Kyle held up a hand. Calluses from years of hard labor covered his palm. He owned a family ranch on the outskirts of Knoxville. "The minute Sierra heard what was going on, she immediately encouraged me to help."

"Addison too. In fact, the ladies will pitch in where they can too. Researching suspects, cooking, and keeping Hayley company." He tossed a smile in her direction. "Our wives have all been in trouble at one time or another and will do everything possible to help you. I'll apologize in advance for what's about to happen."

She laughed. "What will they do?"

"Ply you with baked goods and romantic comedy movies, probably." He rubbed the back of his neck. "Addison's already planning a girls night."

Hayley looked pleased by the idea, and warmth spread through Walker's chest. Today's events had been emotionally draining, but knowing his friends were committed to helping, lifted some of the weight from his shoulders. He wasn't in this alone. "Thanks, guys."

"No thanks necessary." Kyle clapped his shoulder. "Why don't y'all head inside? I'm sure you're exhausted. We can talk more tomorrow and make a definitive game plan." His expression grew serious. "Hopefully, Chief Garcia will have more information by morning."

Walker prayed that was true. If Anna existed, finding her was imperative. Trouble was, he wasn't sure she was real. Casanova's letter could've been designed to upset Hayley enough to send her looking for Walker, setting up an opportunity for him to be shot in front of her. Or tonight had been in retaliation for going to the police against instructions. There was no way to know.

Whatever twisted game Casanova was playing, one thing was certain: Hayley was his obsession. He was coming for her.

Walker would stop him before he did.

He hiked the laptop bag higher on his shoulder. "If you need anything, guys, come inside the house. My mom keeps a fully stocked fridge and pantry."

"We know." Kyle rubbed his stomach. "Your mom already fed lasagna for dinner. She even had brownies for dessert."

The thought of pasta drowning in sauce and cheese made Walker's stomach growl. It was well past dinnertime. From the expression on Hayley's face, she was looking forward to a hot meal too. He placed a hand on the small of her back. "Come on, let's get inside and have something to eat."

With a last wave to his friends, Walker and Hayley climbed the steps to the wide front porch. A swing was nestled in the corner and rocking chairs shifted in the breeze. Wind chimes danced overhead.

Hayley's steps slowed as they approached the door. She worried her bottom lip with her teeth. "Are you sure this is okay with your parents?"

"Positive." Walker had already called his parents and updated them on what was going on. As expected, his mom and dad immediately wanted Hayley to stay on the ranch.

Before Walker could say anything more, the front door swung open, revealing his mother. Aileen Montgomery was a tall woman with a kind face and a mop of curly hair she'd twisted back into some kind of clip. Her blouse was speckled with flour. The scents of cinnamon and vanilla poured through the open door. Boone bolted inside, his nose lifted in appreciation.

"Hayley, honey, it's so good to see you." Aileen embraced Hayley and then ushered her into the warmth of the house. "Walker told me about your mom. I'm so sorry. We weren't aware, or we'd have attended the funeral."

Some of the tension seemed to ease from Hayley's shoulders. "Thank you, Mrs. Montgomery, that's kind of you to say."

"Please, call me Aileen. You're not a teenager anymore." She turned to Walker, her gaze snagging on the scrape caused by dodging a bullet. Worry deepened the lines around her mouth, and she hugged him for a moment longer than normal. "Love you, son."

His heart twisted at the faint tremble in her voice. Aileen was a practical woman, but she loved her children deeply. Losing Lauren had been hardest on her. It hurt Walker to think of his mother worrying about him, but there was nothing he could do to prevent it. He returned her hug. "Love you too, Mom."

When she backed away from the embrace, tears misted her eyes.

The sound of pegs hitting the wooden floor preceded Walker's father into the entryway. Shane Montgomery was burly. Age and years of working in the sun had roughened his skin and thinned his hair. He hefted a cast that went from hip to ankle, aided by a set of crutches.

Aileen planted her hands on her hips. "Shane, you're supposed to be resting."

"Hush, woman. I came to greet our guest." He winked and grinned at Hayley. "Hey there, darlin'. Welcome home."

"Thank you, sir."

His parents' warm greeting didn't surprise Walker. Losing Lauren had caused overwhelming grief initially, but as the years went by, Aileen and Shane had often talked about Hayley. They'd wondered how she was. Uncertainty about whether she wanted to see them prevented Aileen from reaching out. His mom hadn't wanted to intrude on Hayley's healing process. But they'd missed her all the same.

"Now then." Aileen clapped her hands and took Hayley's coat from her, hanging it on a peg next to the door. "Have you had dinner?"

Hayley shook her head, toeing off her sneakers. "No, but I don't want to put you out—"

"Nonsense. You must be starving." Aileen took Hayley's hand and tugged her toward the kitchen before casting a glance over her shoulder. "Walker, can you put the suitcases in the guest room upstairs? Then come join us."

"Will do."

He didn't make a move to pick up the suitcases, sensing his dad wanted to speak to him. Shane waited until Aileen and Hayley disappeared around the corner before the smile fled from his face. He turned a steely gaze toward Walker. "You okay, son? And don't give me any malarkey." Shane straightened, holding the crutches in his hand, until they were eye to eye. "It'll only make me worry more if you sugarcoat matters."

"I'm okay, Dad. The cut looks bad, but it's nothing a bit of over-the-counter pain meds can't take care of. Logan said it's a good thing I'm hardheaded."

That comment earned him a half-smile. Then Shane glanced toward the kitchen before settling his gaze back on Walker. His dark eyes, so much like Lauren's, reflected his concern. "It's Casanova? For sure?"

"It's too early in the investigation to know with certainty, but if you're asking what my gut says..." Walker's fingers twitched with the desire to form a fist. "It's him."

"Why now?"

Walker shrugged. "Hayley came back to town to bury her mother. Maybe her reappearance triggered him." He didn't share his suspicions that Casanova had been actively hunting and killing other women in the interim. He didn't have proof, and it wasn't smart to operate on guesswork. "Chief Garcia is doing everything he can. Ryker's tied up with a double murder case, but once it finishes, he'll assist."

Shane grunted in approval. Ryker didn't live in Knoxville, but he visited as often as he could. Walker's cousin was an experienced Texas Ranger. Having his expertise would go a long way.

"Jason and Kyle will keep watch tonight," Walker continued. "The guys will work in shifts to protect the property closest to the house, and if need be, help work the case. Casanova specifically instructed Hayley not to go to the police. If he's the one who shot at me tonight—and I believe he is—then he's mad that she disobeyed him." He rocked back on his heels. "Adding insult to injury, Casanova missed me when he took potshots. That'll ramp up his temper."

"Maybe he'll make a mistake that'll finally lead to his arrest."

Walker nodded. "We can hope. In the meantime, the ranch hands should be alert for anything suspicious."

"I've already let them know." Shane leaned against his crutches.

Weariness creased his features. "Everyone is aware they should use extra care."

"Good." Walker picked up Hayley's suitcase. "Go back to the recliner, Dad, before Mom fusses at you for being on your feet."

Shane grumbled something about mother hens and being smothered by feathers as he hobbled back into the living room. Walker made sure his dad was settled in the recliner before climbing the stairs to the second floor. Photographs lined the hallway, a montage of Walker and Lauren as they grew up. He deftly avoided looking at them.

The guest bedroom was at the end of the hall. It had once belonged to Walker's grandmother, who'd lived with them for many years after becoming a widow. Now it was reserved for the occasional family member—like Ryker—whenever they passed through town. Walker was also moving into his parents' house, taking his old bedroom down the hall. It'd be easier to protect Hayley and his family if Casanova tried anything.

Walker placed Hayley's suitcases next to the door, noting that his mom had laid out fresh towels on the bed, along with an extra set of toiletries. The blinds on the windows were closed and the ensuite bathroom door was open. Everything was spick and span.

He checked his old bedroom and discovered his mom had put fresh towels on his bed too. Other than that, the room hadn't changed since his teen years. A twin bed and desk took up most of the space. Academic awards sat next to his football trophies on a shelf over the small closet. Walker closed the door.

Across the hall was Lauren's room. He touched the handle but didn't turn it. Walker hadn't been inside since the day she passed. Like his room, nothing had changed. His parents hadn't had the strength to give away her clothes or pack up her belongings. Aileen once let it slip that whenever she was sad, she'd sit in Lauren's room to feel close to her. The image of his mother on his sister's bed, crying, had haunted Walker for months.

"I'll get him, Lauren." Grief thickened his whisper. "I promise you. I'll get him."

The creak of the staircase drew his attention. Hayley stood at the end of the hall, Boone at her side. Her complexion was pale, her mouth drawn tight. She clutched her cell phone in one hand. As if sensing her unease, Boone whimpered.

Walker instantly moved away from Lauren's door. "What is it?"

"He sent another message." Hayley tapped on the screen with a trembling finger before turning the device toward Walker.

It was a picture of them outside the police department, taken moments before the shooting happened. Underneath was a text message.

You disobeyed my instructions. I said don't go to the police.
Now Anna will die.

SEVEN

Hayley shot into a seated position, a scream on her lips.

She wrestled with the arms holding her before realizing she was gripping sheets. A wet nose nudged her hand and then came a whimper. Hayley blinked. The nightmare faded as the room came into focus. Sunlight trickled through gauzy curtains. Lush blue carpeting and a four-poster bed. Boone whimpered again and pressed his large body against hers. She wasn't trapped in a shed fighting off a killer.

She was at Blue Star Ranch, in the guest bedroom.

Safe.

Trembles quaked through Hayley's body and sweat soaked her skin. Boone whimpered again and crept even closer until his heavy body was laying over her legs. He licked her cheek.

A sob rose in Hayley's throat. The nightmare had been awful this time, triggered by recent events. She released the tangle of sheets in her hands to bury her fingers into Boone's soft fur. The scent of his shampoo—something lilac mixed with the earthy smell of the ranch—grounded her. He licked her cheek again, swiping away the tears coursing over her skin, forcing a laugh to bubble up despite the terror of the bad dream. "You're a good dog, Boone. The best."

He gazed at her with soulful eyes. She rubbed his broad head, grateful Walker had insisted on Boone spending the night with her. Hayley hadn't slept much. Every time she closed her eyes, the haunting message Casanova had sent last night kept flashing in her mind.

Now Anna will die.

Hayley understood the message could be an empty threat sent to terrorize her, but last night, in the dark, it was hard to wrestle logic from emotion. She tossed and turned, racking her brain, trying to figure out who Anna could be. To no avail. She didn't know anyone by that name. Hayley had studied the photograph of the bracelet so much, she had it memorized. A search of town residents brought up three women named Anna. A quick text to Chief Garcia confirmed deputies had checked on all of them. The women were fine. None of them recognized the bracelet.

When Hayley finally fell asleep in the early-morning hours, a mixture of visions stalked her dreams. A woman being branded while chained. Casanova's breath, hot on Hayley's face, his gloved hand stroking her cheek. The echo of the gunshot that stole Lauren's life.

And Walker... dying right in front of her eyes.

A new tremble shook Hayley's body, but this time, she battled it back. Sucking in several breaths to slow her heart rate, she willed herself to get a grip on her runaway emotions. Casanova intended to frighten her. He fed off her worry and fear. She refused to give him one more ounce of it. Hayley was a survivor. Tougher than most gave her credit for. She wouldn't hide under the covers and wait for the killer to make his next move.

No, she'd find him. Stop him.

Once and for all.

Hayley gave Boone one last pat and then rose from the bed. Showering erased the last of her nightmares. She dressed in a warm sweater and jeans before heading downstairs, Boone at her side. The rich aroma of coffee mixed with cinnamon teased her senses. She rounded the corner into the sun-filled kitchen to find it empty. A note, written in Aileen's neat hand, rested against a plate of cinnamon rolls.

Sorry to leave before you wake up, but Shane has a doctor's appointment this morning. Please help yourself to anything in the kitchen. I've made these rolls especially for you. I remembered they're your favorite.

Hayley set the note down, a smile playing on her lips and a tender warmth filling her heart. It was followed by a thick cut of sadness coated in grief. Lauren should be here, enjoying her mother's baking. It didn't feel right. Being here without her.

Boone whined at the door. Hayley opened it and the dog shot out into the yard. Despite the steady sunshine, icy precipitation clung to the oak trees and coated the bushes. She made her way to the coffee pot and poured some of the potent brew into a mug. The first sip got her synapses firing.

Twenty minutes later, she'd polished off two cups of coffee and a cinnamon bun. Her belly full, she turned her attention to the fields beyond the large windows in the living room. It was as pretty as a painting. Horses grazed in pastures separated by white fencing. A red barn dotted the landscape. Hayley spotted Walker in the paddocks, working with a black horse. She hated to bother him, but wanted to take another look at the murder board in his house.

The air was crisp outside. Boone raced to greet her as she stepped off the porch. The mutt trotted alongside as Hayley's strides ate up the distance to the barn. Birds chirped overhead. A squirrel scurried down the oak tree and Boone bolted after it. Hayley shook her head at the dog's antics. He had enough energy to power the whole town if they could harness it.

Despite the cold weather, Walker had shed his jacket and rolled his shirtsleeves up to his elbows. A cowboy hat shielded his gaze from the sun. The murmur of his voice drifted on the wind. As Hayley grew closer, she noticed the black horse was malnourished and whip marks crisscrossed his body. His eyes were wide with fear. Walker held out a hand as he drew closer, trying to gently convince the horse to submit.

Hayley stilled near the fence, mesmerized by the exchange. Walker's body language was powerful, but not aggressive. A solid presence. He edged toward the horse, who eyed him with increasing suspicion. Hayley held her breath. She knew intimately what it was like to be touched by Walker. To be comforted by his embrace and soothing nature. From all appearances, the horse needed tender loving care.

Walker's hand nearly touched the horse's muzzle. Inch by inch, he drew closer.

The breeze shifted. The horse must've caught Hayley's scent because his head whirled around and he reared up. Walker lunged out of the way. His body slammed into the unforgiving dirt, but he didn't stay down. He rolled to his feet. The horse bolted to the other side of the paddock and pawed the ground. His breath came in snorts.

Hayley winced and called out, "Sorry."

Walker dusted off his clothes before bending over to retrieve his hat from the dirt. "It's not your fault. Midnight doesn't trust me yet."

"What happened to him?"

"I don't know details, but it's clear he was abused." He joined her at the fence, his gaze still on the horse. "Cassie..." Walker paused. "That's the woman who was here yesterday when you arrived. Her husband, Nathan, is a friend of mine." His lips curled into a wry smile. "Another one of the Special Forces. Nathan is a former Green Beret."

Hayley had gauged him as former military during their brief conversation yesterday next to the horse trailer. The tall broad-shouldered man had carried himself with a rigid posture and a quiet confidence.

"Anyway, Cassie has a horse rehabilitation center," Walker continued. "Midnight's a rescue. Cassie's stables were full, so she asked if he could stay here for a while."

Hayley wasn't surprised by his generosity. Walker had always been unfailingly kind. The first time she noticed him was when he defended a freshman against a pack of bullies. He'd faced down five seniors, and while he took a licking, Walker gave it as good as he got. Hayley had been the one to find a teacher to break things up. She'd also defended Walker to the principal when he was nearly suspended for fighting.

"You'll get through to him." Hayley studied the whip marks along Midnight's flanks. He had a good reason not to trust people. "It'll take time though."

He faced her and flashed a charming grin. "I know."

Her heart stuttered. The man was impossibly handsome. She'd forgotten how easily he could disarm her with a simple look. Memories of laughter and tender kisses flickered through her mind like a montage. She forced them back. Whatever romantic feelings existed between her and Walker were long gone.

Lauren's murder had changed everything.

Hayley tucked her hands into the pockets of her jacket, forcing her gaze away from the handsome cowboy before Walker caught on to her thoughts. She rocked back on her heels. "I keep thinking about the messages from Casanova. Do you mind if I take another look at your murder board? Studying the information again might give me new insight."

"Sure thing." Walker removed his jacket from a fence post and shrugged it on. "I'll come with you. Give me a second to put Midnight out to graze."

He loped away to open a gate on the far end of the paddock. The horse, sensing freedom, bolted for the grassy pasture. He whinnied in pleasure and munched on the grass. Other horses, in a separate area, nickered in greeting and drifted to the fence line. They seemed interested in the latest addition to Blue Star Ranch.

Hayley gestured toward the pasture. "Maybe you should couple Midnight up with another horse. A steady one who trusts you. It might help him adjust and calm down."

"Good idea." Walker closed the gate as he exited the paddocks. "I'll ask Cassie about it. She's Midnight's true owner. I don't want to overstep my bounds."

Considerate. Walker was always considerate. It was another trait of his that drew her like a moth to a flame. She couldn't help the way her heart skipped a beat as he fell into step beside her. Her palm tingled with the urge to take his hand, just like old times. She resisted.

The walk to Walker's house was short. The warmth of the office wiped away the chill from outside, and Hayley dumped her coat in a chair. Boone, who'd followed them, settled into a bed in the corner with a sigh. His long ears flopped against the floor.

She eyed the murder board. The best way to approach this was by starting at the beginning. "Did you check missing person's records to see if brunettes were disappearing before Lauren and I were kidnapped?"

He nodded, perching on the corner of the desk. "I did. There were a few women that went missing in the years prior, but none fit with what I know about Casanova. In my opinion, you and Lauren were his first."

Hayley forced herself to go back to the moment of the carjacking, this time seeing with an investigator's mindset. The crime required planning, but Casanova had made mistakes. He'd been jittery initially and hadn't locked the car doors, which enabled Hayley to attempt to push Lauren out of the vehicle at a stoplight. It hadn't worked. Nor had trying to get the young girl to run once they entered the woods.

Lauren had been frozen with shock and fear.

After Casanova shot her, he held Hayley captive in a shed. He'd secured her with zip ties and locked the building with a padlock. But there had been a hole in the hard plastic siding, close to the cement foundation. It took a few days, but Hayley broke her binds and escaped.

The heart branded on her shoulder burned with a phantom pain. Even that had taken a couple of tries for Casanova to get right. He'd planned it but hadn't executed the procedure like someone who'd done it multiple times before.

Hayley rolled her shoulder to ease the burning sensation. "Yes, I think you're right. Lauren and I were his first victims." She tilted her head and studied the board. "In fact, your sister wasn't supposed to be in the car with me that day. Thinking back on it, her presence surprised him."

"That's probably why he shot her once y'all got to the woods. She wasn't the primary target."

No. Hayley was. Guilt slammed into her like a tidal wave, but she battled it back, forcing herself to focus on the task at hand. She turned her attention to the missing women lined up on the left-hand side of the board. There were eight in total. All of them had disappeared from different jurisdictions.

She waved a finger over them. "Let's assume you're right, Walker, and Casanova kidnapped these other victims. None of them are from Knoxville."

"It would be easier for law enforcement to link the cases if they were all in the same jurisdiction."

"Agreed. Casanova's smart. Killing Lauren and kidnapping me made him famous, but it also put him at risk of being caught. He doesn't want to go to prison. So he broadens his hunting ground." She came to a stop in front of the map. "But that doesn't change one simple fact: He's from here. Casanova stalked me. He knows me. Knoxville is his home, and likely, I've run into him somewhere."

The image of the pearl bracelet flashed in her mind. "Let's also assume Anna is a real person. Casanova expects me to figure out who she is." An idea formed in Hayley's mind, and her breath caught. She pointed to the location of Knoxville High School. "His original hunting ground isn't the town."

Walker shot straight up. "It's the high school."

EIGHT

Knoxville High School was located on a country road surrounded by fields of grazing cattle. The parking lot was a mix of jalopies, trucks, and sedans. Marching band practice was underway, students stepping in sync, the sound of an out-of-tune tuba carrying on the wind. Several other students lingered outside the theater sharing a bag of potato chips. A security guard circled the parking lot in a golf cart.

Nothing was out of the ordinary. Still the hairs on the back of Walker's neck stood on end as he opened the passenger-side door of the truck for Hayley. There were eyes on them. "You feel that?"

She nodded. Her sharp-eyed gaze scanned the area before she exited the vehicle. "Can't tell where it's coming from." Hayley shrugged her shoulders. "Then again, we could be imagining things. We're both jumpy."

They were, and for good reason. Last night, they'd both been shot at.

Walker debated the wisdom of following up on this lead on their own, but a phone call to his buddy Tucker confirmed there weren't any officers free at the moment to take care of it. A pileup on the freeway had resulted in numerous injuries and required a multi-agency response. It would be hours—if not another day—before someone from the police department could come by the high school to ask about the bracelet.

Hayley wasn't willing to wait. Neither was Walker.

The high school was a weapons-free zone. He didn't like leaving his handgun behind, but Walker didn't have a choice. Hayley set her Glock next to his inside the special safe under the driver's-side seat. The hum of a golf cart came up behind Walker.

"Hayley Barlow, is that you?" The security guard hit the brakes and hopped out. Grinning from ear to ear, he enveloped Hayley in a bear hug. "It's been ages."

Recognition zipped through Walker. Chris Wallaby. A former classmate who used to run with the tough crowd. In fact, Walker had gotten into a scuffle while defending a freshman from a pack of seniors. Chris had been one of the bullies. Months later, he apologized to both Walker and the kid he'd bullied, explaining he was going through a hard time and had fallen in with the wrong crowd.

True to his word, Chris turned his behavior around. He and Walker became friendly, although Chris was especially fond of Hayley. Walker always suspected his former nemesis had a thing for the dark-haired beauty. The exuberant greeting the man gave her now reinforced the idea.

"Hey, Chris." Hayley disentangled herself from the security guard's embrace but kept a friendly hand on his arm. She'd never had an interest in him romantically and treated him as she would any other good friend. "It's nice to see you. How have you been?"

He shrugged, tossing a lock of dirty blond hair out of his eyes. His cheeks hadn't lost their youthful chubbiness, although he was sporting a goatee that offset it. "Same old, same old. Trying to keep the bills paid." Sympathy darkened his eyes. "I'm sorry about your mom. Stopped by the house the other day, but you were out. I worked the day of the funeral or I would've been there."

"Thanks for thinking of me."

"Of course." His gaze drifted to Walker, and he gave a nod. Then shifted his attention back to Hayley. "What brings you here? Visiting for old times' sake?"

"Actually, I'm trying to locate the owner of this bracelet. It's possible she works here at the school." Hayley pulled up the photograph on her phone and showed it to Chris. "Have you ever seen it before?"

He studied it, but no flash of recognition crossed his features. He shook his head. "No, but ask Mrs. Haverstein." Chris's mouth tilted in a smile. "Not much gets by that old gal."

"Great, thanks." Hayley gave a wave. "See you later."

"Yeah, let's grab a coffee or something before you leave town." Chris climbed back inside his golf cart. "See ya later."

He drove off with a wave.

Walker watched him go, his mind whirling. "Do you think Chris could be Casanova?"

"Chris?" Shock flickered across Hayley's face and then her brows dipped in thought. "I don't think so. He's had a crush on me since high school, but never been weird about it. I explained that I didn't share his feelings early on. He took it well."

"Or he pretended to take it well." Walker made a mental note to do a background check on Chris. "The guy seems genuine, but a killer like Casanova would be adept at hiding in plain sight."

"Good point."

They crossed the parking lot to the main entrance. The school was unbearably warm inside. Walker immediately unzipped his jacket. A bell rang. The thunderous sound of hundreds of feet pouring out of classrooms was accompanied by loud voices. Lockers slammed. The front office was located a short distance away, nestled between two hallways. One was for juniors. The other for seniors. The freshman and sophomore lockers were located upstairs. A sign stretched across the senior hall announcing ticket sales for the Valentine's Day dance were underway. The theme was famous couples.

A memory wormed its way into his thoughts. Dancing cheek to cheek with Hayley during the homecoming dance at the beginning of their senior year. She'd been stunning in a red dress with a glittery bodice and tulle skirt. If Walker remembered correctly, she'd found the gown at a consignment shop in town. It'd fit her like a glove. She'd been stunning.

Hayley glanced at him out of the corner of her eye and their gazes met for half a moment. Her cheeks pinkened. Suddenly, the surrounding noise fell away as Walker realized she was thinking about the same dance. Their first kiss had been that night. Tentative, but tender. Sweet. He'd driven home on cloud nine.

It was almost painful to remember how young and innocent they'd been back then.

Hayley picked up her pace, reaching the office door before him. Gloria Haverstein glanced up as they entered. She wore a silk blouse buttoned to her throat, reading glasses perched on the end of a haughty nose. Her gray hair was tucked into a bun. Watery blue eyes skimmed over Hayley without a flicker of recognition, but halted when they reached Walker. Her pursed mouth relaxed into a smile. Gloria stood. "Well, as I live and breathe, if it isn't Walker Montgomery. How are you?"

He flashed the older woman a charming smile. As part of his punishment for fighting the bullies, he'd been required to help in the office after school. It'd been a good deal. The principal had originally wanted to suspend him. "Mrs. Haverstein, you haven't aged a day." Walker pointed to the wall lined with inboxes. One for each teacher. "Still running the office as efficiently as ever, I see. Not a paper out of place."

Gloria preened under his compliment. Organization was her love language.

"You remember Hayley Barlow, don't you?" Walker gestured in her direction. "She graduated the same year I did."

Confusion creased her features for a moment before they

smoothed out into a welcoming smile. "Of course, I do. Hayley was nearly our salutatorian." Her smile faltered, as if Gloria remembered the reason Hayley hadn't attended graduation. After Casanova's attack, she dropped out of school and got her GED. "It's been a long time, dear."

"Yes, ma'am, it has."

A door opened behind Mrs. Haverstein. Richard Westbrook, the principal, stepped into the reception area. Years ago, he'd been the algebra teacher but had gradually moved into administration. The local paper did a full-page spread on him when he became principal last year.

Richard was married to a local shop owner and had a daughter in junior high. Closing in on forty, his age was showing with the beginnings of a pot belly and a receding hairline. Walker had never liked the man much. In all fairness, algebra had been his least favorite subject.

"Mr. Westbrook, look at who's come to see us." Gloria beamed like a peacock, showing off its plume of feathers. "It's Walker Montgomery and Hayley Barlow."

Richard's brows arched slightly. His attention zeroed in on Hayley and lingered in a faintly creepy way that turned Walker's insides. A smile played on his thin lips. "Of course, I remember Ms. Barlow. She was one of my favorite students."

The words were meant to be kind—a teacher greeting a top student with fondness—but it came off as slimy. Walker glanced at Hayley. She was staring at Richard, holding his eye-contact, but her shoulders were tense.

She didn't like Richard any more than Walker did. He racked his brains, trying to remember if Hayley had ever had an issue with the former math teacher, but came up blank. Maybe she hadn't told him. Hayley was good at holding in things that bothered her.

Walker stepped closer to her. Placed a hand on the small of her back. A subtle but obvious hint to the other man to cut it out. Hayley leaned into the touch slightly. Just enough to let Walker know that she'd picked up on Richard's weird vibe and appreciated the protection.

Richard's gaze shifted to Walker. Something flashed in his expression before it smoothed out. He nodded. "Mr. Montgomery, nice to see you. I'm sure your family is happy to have you back home again. You were in the Navy last I heard."

"Yes, sir."

"Well, thank you for your service."

Once again, the expression was meant to be kind, but it came out with a slightly mocking edge to it. Walker's internal alarms blared more. He couldn't make sense of why this man unsettled him so much. Richard had never been his favorite teacher in school, but this veiled hostility was new. Or maybe Walker was just older and wiser now. Able to recognize what had been there all along.

"Now what brings you two in for a visit?" Gloria's gaze skipped between the two of them. She seemed oblivious to Richard's strange behavior. "Do you need transcripts?"

"No, ma'am." Hayley pulled out her cell phone from her jacket pocket and accessed the photograph of the bracelet. "Actually, I was hoping you might help me with something. Do either of you recognize this bracelet?"

Richard drew closer to Gloria, and the pair leaned over to examine the photograph.

Walker watched the principal's expression closely, and a flash of recognition crossed his soft features. "That looks like Julianna Clovers's bracelet, doesn't it, Mrs. Haverstein? The clasp broke a few weeks ago, and you repaired it for her."

Hayley stiffened. Walker's heart picked up speed. Julianna Clovers. Was Anna a nickname? It made sense, and he mentally berated himself for not thinking of it earlier.

Gloria nodded. "Of course, yes. You're right, Richard, that is Julianna's bracelet. I knew it looked familiar. She was devastated when the clasp broke. The bracelet was a gift from her mother, who died when Julianna was a little girl." She glanced at Hayley with curiosity. "Do you have the bracelet? I hate to think she lost it again."

"I know where it is, and I'd like to return it to her." Hayley's statement wasn't a lie, but it skirted the truth. "Is she here now?"

"No, Julianna is on maternity leave. She had the most precious little girl..." Gloria's face screwed up. "Oh, I'd say about a month ago."

Maternity leave? Walker's stomach dropped to his feet before leaping back to his throat. That didn't fit with Casanova's MO, but killers evolved. "Do you have Julianna's address?"

Richard frowned at the sharpness in Walker's tone. "I don't believe we can give that information out—"

"It's very important." Walker focused on Gloria. There were other ways to find Julianna's address—Tucker could look it up for them or she might be registered in the town directory—but both options would take time. And neither was a guarantee. "Trust me."

The older woman hesitated, and then she scribbled something down on a sheet of paper. "I was at her home last week, dropping off a baby gift. Julianna is a single mom. Her husband was killed in a car accident last fall."

Walker couldn't process everything she said. He grabbed the paper from her hand and, with a hurried thanks, bolted for the door. Hayley followed, hot on his heels. They burst out of the school into the icy air. Walker barely felt it.

In seconds, he had Tucker on the line. "We've got a name. Julianna Clovers." He rambled off the address while simultaneously unlocking his truck. He hopped into the driver's seat and fired up the engine. "Hayley and I are heading there now."

He peeled out of the parking lot, barely registering that Tucker was sending officers to the address. Julianna lived five minutes from the school. Walker would beat any law enforcement there. He raced through a yellow light and pushed down on the gas pedal.

Please, God. Let her be all right.

It was possible Julianna was alive and being held captive in her own house. Casanova was working from a game plan they didn't understand. There was no way to predict the killer's movements. In the passenger seat beside him, Hayley murmured prayers. Why that made Walker feel better, he couldn't say. All he knew was that it did.

They didn't utter a word between them until Walker pulled into Julianna's driveway. His phone beeped with a text message from Tucker.

"Law enforcement is another ten minutes out." He opened his door, got out, and then pressed his finger to the fingerprint reader on the safe under his seat. It popped open. He handed Hayley her Glock before slipping his own weapon into its holster. "I'm not waiting."

"We can't break into her house."

"No, but we can knock on the door," Walker retorted.

He jogged up the driveway. Julianna's house was a small one-story with a cookie-cutter front stoop. Hanging plants flanked the door, and a welcome mat rested against the concrete. He hit the doorbell with enough force to break it in two. Chimes rang inside.

Hayley joined him on the stoop. She leaned over and peeked into the window facing the street. "The curtains are sheer, but I don't see any movement." Her head tilted to the side. "Do you hear that? It sounds like a baby crying."

Walker hit the doorbell again, and when there was still no response, he pounded on the wood.

The door popped open. The baby's wails grew frantic.

He glanced at Hayley. The latch on the door hadn't caught properly, which is why it popped open when Walker pounded on it. Had someone left in a rush? Or had Julianna simply not closed the door properly? The baby's cries were heart-wrenching, and there was no sound of any movement inside. He couldn't imagine a mother leaving her infant to wail like that.

Nerves coiled his inside. He palmed the center of the door and opened it farther. "Mrs. Clovers, are you home? My name is Walker Montgomery. I need to speak to you, ma'am."

No response, save for the baby. The curtains were drawn in the house, but a playpen in the living room was visible. Walker stepped over the threshold. He risked getting arrested for trespassing. It didn't matter. The vision of a woman bound somewhere inside flooded through his mind. He couldn't wait.

"Mrs. Clovers." His voice carried through the house. "Hello? Anyone home?"

Hayley crossed the room and picked up the red-faced infant. She cuddled her close, murmuring words of comfort. The child stuffed a fist in its mouth. A girl, judging from the pink bunny pajamas. Hungry. She tossed the hand out of her mouth and wailed again before returning to suck on her fist.

Hayley frowned. "Her diaper is sopping and has leaked onto her clothes. She hasn't been changed in a while."

Walker took in the living room. It was tidy. A small couch faced an older television. Several baby toys were stacked in a tub in the corner. There was no sign of a struggle, but something felt off. Very off. The house was eerily quiet.

"Walker."

Hayley's voice was barely above a whisper. His gaze snapped to her and then followed the line of her arm as she pointed at the edge of the baby's playpen.

A heart charm wrapped around a rose had been hung from the side like a talisman.

Casanova. The man had a twisted fascination with hearts. He'd even branded one onto Hayley's left shoulder. And he'd left roses for her after breaking into her mom's house. Walker's internal warning system blared. "Take the baby outside to the truck, lock the doors, and call Tucker. Give him an update. I'll search the rest of the house."

Hayley nodded and rushed from the room. He waited until she

was secure in the vehicle before rounding the corner into the kitchen. Empty. He turned and crossed the living room toward the hallway leading to the bedroom. He kept his hand on his weapon but didn't pull it. If Julianna was here, and in the shower or something, his presence alone would be enough to frighten the poor woman.

Walker didn't think that was likely though. Still... "Mrs. Clovers?"

No answer. The house was warm, the heater running on full blast to ward off the February chill. Sweat beaded on Walker's forehead as a familiar smell twisted his memories.

Blood.

Dread slowed his steps as he entered the small bedroom tucked in the rear of the house. The curtains were drawn in this room too, but the bed was neatly made. Nearby, within reaching distance, was a cradle. Tennis shoes lined the area in front of a dresser. The closet door was open, a few clothes hanging inside. No sign of Julianna.

The bathroom door was cocked open. Walker pushed it with his foot. A hand was visible hanging from the bathtub. Mentally, he knew she was gone, but an illogical hope kept him moving forward. His boots slid over the tile floor as he edged closer to the tub.

Julianna Clovers lay on her side, lifeless eyes staring at the wall. A heart had been branded onto her shoulder and a typewritten note pinned to her shirt.

Remember what I'm capable of.

NINE

The next evening, Hayley tucked a blanket around little Sophia as she rested in the crib. The infant was three weeks old with a swatch of dark hair and wide blue eyes. Her sweet mouth puckered in her sleep. Did she know her mother had been taken from her?

God, there are some things I don't understand.

Hayley's fingers touched the tattoo on her wrist, a reminder that the good Lord had spared her. But why not Julianna? Or Lauren? It was a question she'd never have an adequate answer to, which was a bitter pill to swallow. Layered on top was the perpetual feeling that this was all her fault somehow. Mentally, Hayley understood Casanova was to blame, but his obsession with her had set this entire thing in motion. A sense of responsibility plagued her.

The hours after discovering Julianna's body were a blur of answering police questions and waiting at the hospital for news about Sophia. Hayley and Walker didn't return to the ranch until late in the evening. This morning, Hayley began reviewing every scrap of information Walker had collected over the last two years. It was extensive.

Twelve hours later, she was exhausted but more determined than ever to find Casanova and stop him. The man deserved to rot in prison for his crimes.

Hayley checked her watch. She had half an hour. Walker's friends—the Special Forces—were on their way to the ranch. Tucker had news about the investigation to share and they were going to brainstorm suspects. Hayley wasn't the only one determined to solve the case. They all were.

Each member of the Special Forces had spoken to her privately at some point last night or today, checking on her well-being. The men weren't pushy or nosy. They allowed Hayley to talk—or not—as much as she liked. Walker had been right about them. They were unfailingly supportive.

Sophia sighed, her little mouth moving in a sucking motion. The emergency room doctor had given her a complete physical. Infants weren't supposed to go over six hours without eating. The coroner estimated Julianna had been murdered shortly after Hayley received the message from Casanova, which meant the baby had gone almost twelve hours without food. She'd been dehydrated, which was deadly for anyone, but especially for a baby so young. Discovering Julianna's identity and their quick actions once arriving at the house had likely saved Sophia's life.

It was something to be grateful for.

Aileen slipped into the room, carrying extra baby blankets and burp cloths. She laid them on the white dresser next to a window overlooking the back side of the ranch. The baby's room was downstairs, in a small alcove next to the primary bedroom. Social services had placed the infant with Walker's parents for the time being. A wise decision, one the chief of police strongly supported, since it meant Sophia was protected by a group of former military men.

The rose and heart left on the baby's playpen was haunting. Casanova had left Sophia alone after murdering her mom, and it seemed a long shot that he'd come back for the baby, but better to be safe than sorry.

"How's she doing?" Aileen's voice was hushed as she joined Hayley. A smile spread across the older woman's face. "I'd almost forgotten how tiny newborn babies are. She's nothing but a spot in the crib."

It was true. Hayley had almost no experience with babies, but she couldn't imagine how anyone wouldn't fall in love with Sophia at first sight. She was precious. "Watching Sophia sleep is peaceful. It's like everything is right in the world."

Aileen nodded. "I couldn't have said it better myself."

"What will happen to her?"

"The social worker is looking for extended family. Julianna has cousins up north somewhere. Hopefully, they'll be able to care for little Sophia." She placed a hand on Hayley's arm. "How are you holding up, hon? The last few days have been a lot, especially after losing your mom."

"I'm hanging in there. Just needed a minute to escape everything." She peeked at the older woman out of the corner of her eye. "I've brought a heap of trouble to your doorstep."

"Nonsense. I know we haven't spoken in a long time, not since Lauren's death, but there's something very important you need to know. Our door is always open. Always. I'm glad you came to us when you were in trouble. We care about you and it's an honor to provide you with a soft place to land."

Unbidden tears sprang to Hayley's eyes. She'd missed the Montgomery family. Spending time with them again was unearthing all the memories she'd worked hard to bury after leaving Knoxville. Hayley had spent nearly every day on the ranch during her senior year.

Her home had been unpredictable. There were times her mother was functional enough to work, but then her addiction would spiral out of control again. It was a rotating door of stress and confusion. Hayley had often escaped to her grandmother's—Nana had been the one to raise her, but passed when Hayley was sixteen—and then to the Montgomery's. Their home was everything she wanted for herself. Loving, supportive, and fun. A glimpse at what life was supposed to be like.

Hayley bit her lip, wrestling her emotions back under control. "I thought... I would've reached out sooner, but I thought Lauren's death would change the way you feel."

"Oh hon, I'm sorry. That's not the case at all." Aileen squeezed her arm. "I didn't contact you because I figured when you left town that you didn't want any reminders of what had happened. But you've been in my prayers every night. Shane's too." She shook her head slightly, her lips thinning. "I'm a foolish woman. I should've realized you needed to hear from me. After Lauren died, I was a wreck for months. It took time to put the pieces back together, and by then, you were gone. Still, that's no excuse. You were only a child."

Warmth unfurled in Hayley's chest. She hugged Aileen. "There's no need to apologize. We both made assumptions about the other. There's no handbook on how to handle the tragedy we went through."

"Ain't that the truth." Aileen pulled back. Tears misted her eyes. She gave Hayley a watery smile. "I'm glad we talked."

"Me too."

Movement in the doorway interrupted the tender moment. Walker appeared, Boone at his side. His gaze shifted between the two women, concern creasing his handsome brow. "Sorry to interrupt. Everything okay?"

His mom nodded. "Fine, son."

Hayley tried to discreetly swipe at the tears on her cheeks, but failed miserably. A whimper came from the crib. Sophia blinked her large eyes and then let out a mewing cry. Inside the swaddle, her little hands and feet shifted.

Aileen scooped her up. "Sweet girl, are you hungry? It's time for your bottle. Yes, it is."

She drifted out of the nursery, still murmuring to the baby.

Walker studied Hayley for a long moment, his gaze sweeping over her face. He lifted a hand and swiped a thumb across her cheek. "You were crying. Are you sure everything is okay?"

Her breath caught. Walker's touch was meant to be comforting, but it sent a wave of heat through her skin. A flush crept up her neck. Once again, Hayley wrestled with her emotions. Walker was standing close enough she could take one step into his arms. It was tempting.

"I'm okay." She sighed. "You were right. Your mom and dad don't blame me for what happened to Lauren."

"Of course not. It wasn't your fault." He held her gaze. "And neither is what happened to Julianna."

She turned away from him and went to the window. Darkness had fallen, but LED lights were strategically placed along walkways and in bushes to illuminate the yard. Oak trees dotted the landscape, and the barn was visible. Hayley hugged her arms around her midsection. "It's hard not to feel responsible."

Walker was quiet for a long moment. She felt rather than heard him come up behind her. Then it was his turn to sigh, long and low. "I know what you mean. You replay the events over and over again, believing that if you'd just done one thing differently, then..."

"Julianna would still be alive. And Lauren."

She turned to face him. The pain he kept hidden most of the time was there in the curve of his lips and the crease of his brow. Hayley's heart ached. She'd suspected Walker blamed himself for Lauren's death—the man had a murder board in his house—but hearing him admit it twisted her insides in a new way.

Hayley couldn't stop herself from wrapping her arms around his waist. The move was familiar, something she'd done while they were dating. So much time had passed and yet it felt as natural as breathing to touch him. "You aren't responsible for their deaths either. Just in case you needed someone to say it out loud."

He pulled her closer, enveloping Hayley in his strong embrace.

His flannel shirt was soft against her cheek. The steady sound of his heartbeat was soothing. She breathed in, the scent of his laundry soap and something distinctively Walker, wrapped around her like a comforting blanket. His chin rested against the crown of her head. The tension eased from her muscles.

How long they stood there, Hayley couldn't say. She didn't care. Both of them needed this, needed each other.

She lifted her face. Walker's gaze was soft as he brushed a strand of hair from her forehead. He gently tucked it behind Hayley's ear, the sweep of his fingers blazing a trail of heat across her skin. A delicious tension coiled in her belly.

Their gazes locked. A myriad of emotions tumbled through Hayley, too many to understand or catalog. This man... he'd been her first love. Her first kiss. Last week, they'd been in different states, living separate lives. It seemed like another lifetime.

But it wasn't. Tragedy and heartbreak separated them. Casanova's attack and Lauren's murder only proved what Hayley already knew long before those events tore her and Walker apart.

She wasn't good enough for him. Never had been. Never would be.

Walker came from a family full of love. Honesty, integrity, and loyalty was the code he lived by. His mother made him breakfast before school, his dad helped with his math homework, and their home was warm and inviting. Literally, a white picket fence surrounded the property.

She grew up half-feral. Running through the woods barefoot, picking berries to eat from bushes because her mom was passed out on the couch. Fixing meals by herself—when she could find food to eat—and doing her own laundry. Law enforcement had been called to her house more than once. One kind neighbor showed Hayley how to tip her mom on her side when she vomited after binge drinking. She'd been six.

Her grandmother had done her best to pick up the slack, but

Nana suffered from debilitating back pain after an auto accident. There were days she could barely take care of herself, let alone Hayley.

She and Walker came from different worlds, and while it was possible to bridge the gap for a while, it couldn't last a lifetime. Things would fall apart.

Hayley backed out of his embrace. Her rear hit the windowsill. "Walker... things are complicated between us. It's probably not smart to add to the trouble already on our plate." She gave him a wry smile. "You and I have always had a connection. That's never going to change, but..."

He breathed out. "It's a distraction. One we don't need."

"Yeah. Our focus needs to be on finding and catching Casanova. Once that's done, I'm selling my mom's house and cutting ties with this town. Knoxville holds too many bad memories for me."

That was only half true. Blue Star Ranch held some of her happiest memories, but she didn't want to open that particular can of worms. It wouldn't help. Walker deserved a wife who wasn't... for lack of a better word... broken.

Her future wasn't here with Walker. It was better to make that clear now before one—or both of them—ended up hurt.

He scraped a hand through his hair. "You're right. We need to keep our attention on the mission." Walker met her gaze in the dim room and his lips tilted into a smile. "Do your best to keep your hands to yourself, Hails. I know I'm irresistible and all, but find a way."

She rolled her eyes and laughed. "Whatever." She pushed him playfully. "We both know *you* were about to kiss *me*."

"That's not how I remember it."

Boone nudged Hayley's hand, and she patted him on the head. "Even your dog is taking my side."

"He's an unreliable witness who can be bought with hotdogs and doggie biscuits."

They both laughed, any lingering tension evaporating away.

Hayley was glad they'd talked. Clearing the air was always better in her opinion, and the last thing she wanted was to hurt Walker.

Her cell phone rang. Hayley pulled it from her pocket and stiffened. The phone number flashing across her screen was local but not one she recognized. "Walker, I think this is Casanova." She quickly pulled up an app to record the call and then answered it. "Hello."

"You messed up, sweetheart."

Casanova's drawl poured from her phone speaker, filling the nursery with his presence. It sucked the air out of the room. Walker's expression was fierce, his hands balled into fists. It looked like he wanted to snatch the cell from Hayley's hand and throw it against the wall. For some ridiculous reason, his protectiveness shored up her strength.

"I told you not to involve the police." He tsked. "You should've listened. If you had, Anna would still be alive today."

Anna. Casanova called the woman by the name on her bracelet. Why? Had he known her personally? Was he related to her? Or was that designed to throw Hayley and the other investigators off?

She tucked that tidbit away and quickly calculated several responses. He wanted to feed her guilt and fear. She wouldn't allow it. "You would've killed Julianna no matter what I did."

He chuckled. Actually chuckled. It sent a white hot rage shooting through Hayley's veins.

She did her best to tamp it down and sound bored. "What do you want?"

"You know what I want."

"Yeah, yeah. Me." She was poking him. Purposefully. If Casanova was focused on her, then he wouldn't be stalking unsuspecting women. "Then come and get me, you coward. Let's go head–to-head and see who comes out on top this time."

"You always were feisty, sweetheart." He sounded amused by her response. "Don't worry, we'll be together soon enough. But we aren't done playing the game yet."

Her heart skittered. She met Walker's eyes and her own worst fears were reflected back.

Casanova wasn't done killing.

Hayley's hand tightened on the phone until her fingers turned white. "Good try, but I'm not playing any stupid game with you."

"Yes, you will. I've watched you, Hayley. For a long time. You care about people, even those you've never met. It's your weakness and it'll be your undoing." He chuckled. "This time, I would follow the rules though. No police. Just you and me and Walker."

"Why Walker?"

"He's been looking for me. It's amusing."

Casanova intended to appear nonchalant, but there was an underlying thread of anger buried in his voice. It jiggled some buried memory in the back of Hayley's mind. Before she could latch onto it, the thought was gone. Hayley gritted her teeth and fought for control of her tone. "You shouldn't have killed Julianna. The police won't stop trying to solve her murder. Your days are numbered."

"Ooooo, now I'm scared." Casanova was in control and he knew it. Relished it. "Don't ignore my instructions again, sweetheart, or I won't just kill the next woman, I'll torture her." He paused for a moment. "When you look in the mirror and see the heart on your shoulder, do you think of me? I know you do."

Hayley's body shook. Not with fear. With rage. "I'm going to lock you in a prison cell."

"Not if I kill you first," he retorted. "I'll be in touch soon with your next clue. Until then, sweet dreams."

Casanova hung up.

TEN

An hour later, Casanova's words haunted Walker. They'd sent the recording to Chief Garcia immediately. No one had been reported missing, but the threat was clear. The killer had already selected his next victim, and the clock was ticking.

Not just for some yet-unnamed woman. For Hayley too.

Casanova was obsessed with her. One of the hardest things Walker had ever done was stand in the nursery and listen to the killer torment her with his words. He wanted to hunt the man down and rip him limb from limb. Walker wasn't a vigilante, nor did he believe in using unnecessary violence—he was a Christian, after all—but there were times his temper got the better of his thoughts.

It'd taken prayer, a hard run, and a cold shower to allow for rational thought to take hold. Hayley had joined him for the run, keeping pace with him easily, and Walker sensed her own temper was frayed. Now, she seemed calmer and more in control as they trudged down the path from the main house to Walker's smaller one. His friends were already there, gathered together to discuss the case.

An owl hooted overhead. Walker tucked his hands in the pockets of his jacket. Casanova's call wasn't the only thing that'd rocked his emotions. He'd come close to kissing Hayley earlier in the evening. The memory batted around his brain like a ping-pong ball. Walker peeked at her, and his heart skipped a beat.

The night air had put a flush in her cheeks. Strands of her gorgeous hair peeked out from underneath a knit cap. No makeup. Moonlight kissed her features, highlighting the curve of her cheeks and the line of her nose. She was, in one word, breathtaking. The only thing more phenomenal than her looks was her inner beauty.

Hayley had strength. More than anyone else he'd ever met. She'd taken what happened with Casanova and used it to fuel her faith. That alone was admirable. But Hayley was so much more than just the tragedy she'd endured. She was also generous and unfailingly kind. Intelligent. Fiercely determined to stand up for what was right. It was a powerful combination, and Walker had almost forgotten what it was like to be in her presence hour after hour. Like a magnet, he was drawn into her orbit.

He needed to be careful. Walker suspected, if he was truly honest with himself, that he'd never gotten over Hayley. She wasn't the type of woman any man forgot. But he'd changed. Time and life experiences had hardened him. Lauren's murder and Hayley's kidnapping had been Walker's first brush with violence. It wasn't his last. Joining the Navy SEALs and deploying to war zones had ripped away the last remnants of his idealism. Walker was intimately familiar with how life could change in a single breath. The world narrowed to a moment. Then the next. It became futile to plan for anything beyond survival. And then, at some point, he simply stopped planning any kind of future at all. It was too painful.

Life was unpredictable. Anything could happen.

Even after returning home, Walker avoided thinking about anything too far in advance. He'd buried himself in ranch work and finding Lauren's killer. Dating was a non-starter. He couldn't wrap his mind around the idea of marriage and children. Then Hayley burst into his life again, and within a few days, he was questioning everything he knew. It was unsettling.

The smell of fresh coffee and a cacophony of voices greeted Walker when he stepped into his small house. Everyone was gathered in the kitchen. Someone had removed the corkboard from his office. It leaned against the large window, visible from every place in the room. Pie boxes, Nelson's Diner scrawled across the front, littered the kitchen table.

Hayley shrugged off her jacket, and the guys greeted her like a long-lost sister. Within moments, she had a cup of coffee in her hand and Kyle was offering her a piece of cherry cobbler. Walker had mentioned to his friend it was her favorite earlier in the day.

"Harriet and Nelson are still in business?" Hayley's eyes shone with happiness.

"Yep. With no sign of stopping." Kyle wrangled a generous piece of cobbler onto a plate. The cherries were ruby red, the topping baked to a golden brown. Nelson's Diner was located on a country road frequented by truckers, weary travelers, and locals. The building itself looked run-down and sketchy, but the homemade pies were the best in Texas. "You should stop by if you get a chance. I mentioned to Harriet that you were in town and she was overjoyed. Said you were the best waitress she'd ever had."

Hayley blushed. "She exaggerates. But I'll stop by the diner before leaving town."

Walker poured himself a cup of coffee and claimed the chair next to Hayley. He peeked in several of the boxes, looking for a lemon meringue. Logan, dressed for the evening shift in his paramedics uniform, his hair damp from a recent shower, gestured toward the lone pie on the counter. "Yours is over there."

Walker grinned. None of the other guys liked that flavor, which meant more pie for him. Walker cut a piece and dug in. The tangy lemon mixed with the crisp meringue to create an explosion of flavor in his mouth. "Y'all are missing out. This is the best pie."

Hayley dipped her fork into his slice and lifted it to her mouth. Her nose wrinkled. "Uh, no. That's gross." She shuddered. "It's like licking a lemon."

Laughter followed her statement. The guys congratulated Hayley on having good taste and ribbed Walker. He threw a few verbal jabs back. Hayley's laughter rang out like a peal of bells. Her cheeks were smushed from smiling, and her eyes sparkled. It warmed Walker's heart. She'd only known the guys for a few days but, somehow, had slipped into the group with ease.

She was amazing. And once again, Walker fell victim to the immutable attraction humming between them. His body leaned closer to her. Hayley smiled in his direction, her eyes warm with good humor. Walker's heart fluttered, and it took every ounce of his willpower to avoid looking at her lips. Instead, he forced himself to sit back in the chair.

Across the table, Jason eyed him knowingly. The former Marine was the quietest member of the group. And the most observant. Walker discreetly shook his head to signal his feelings for Hayley weren't up for discussion. He shoved another piece of pie into his mouth. Every member of their group had become ensnared in protecting a woman from danger and fallen in love along the way.

Walker was the last man standing. The only single one in the group. That aspect didn't bother him at all, and if it'd been any other woman, there wouldn't be a problem protecting her without involving his heart. But Hayley... she was different. Always had been. Walker was deluding himself to think it'd be easy to keep her at arm's length. But he needed to. Hayley had no intention of staying in Knoxville and she'd made that clear... good grief... thirty minutes ago.

He needed to keep his head straight and focus on the mission. Julianna's murder had brought the stakes to a new level, and Casanova's phone call erased any doubts about his plan. He intended to kill again. They had to stop him.

Hayley's life depended on it.

With that sobering thought, Walker pushed his empty plate away and held up a hand. "I hate to break up the fun, but we should get down to business." He stood and went to the corkboard leaning against the window. Everyone at the table grew serious, their grim faces reflecting his own feelings. "I'll give a short rundown of what we have so far to get us all on the same page. Ten years ago, Hayley and my sister Lauren were carjacked by a masked man known only as Casanova. He forced the women to drive to a secluded area. Casanova shot Lauren and held Hayley captive for days."

He cast an apologetic glance in her direction. None of this could be easy for Hayley to hear. But she didn't flinch or shy away. She lifted her chin and gave a subtle nod, encouraging him to go on.

"Casanova used a cattle brand to sear a heart into Hayley's shoulder. She escaped the shed and later led police back to the location, but the building had been burned to the ground. The property Hayley was held on belonged to Thomas Daniels. He was questioned repeatedly by police, but the section of land where the shed was hadn't been used by the family for years. It was overgrown. Thomas claimed anyone could have snuck onto that section of his property without him knowing. The police couldn't refute that claim. As a result, no charges were ever filed. Thomas committed suicide two years later."

"The police chief at the time assured me that Thomas was Casanova," Hayley added. "He didn't have enough evidence to arrest him, but was confident the threat was over. So was I."

"I wasn't." Walker's gaze settled on the photographs on the opposite side of the corkboard. "Since returning home, I've been quietly investigating my sister's murder. While searching for similar cases, I discovered several women had disappeared from surrounding counties." He pointed to the pictures. "These women were kidnapped off the street or disappeared with their vehicles, suggesting they were carjacked. They range in ages from 25 to 40, single, and brunette. Each of them bears a striking resemblance to Hayley."

Nathan crossed his arms over his chest. The sleeves on his shirt strained with the movement. He was no longer a Green Beret, but hadn't lost a single ounce of muscle since leaving the military. Dog tags hung around his neck. "Is it your assertion that Casanova kidnapped these women?"

Walker nodded. "I think he held them someplace, like he did with Hayley, and then eventually killed them before burying their bodies. Probably on private property, which is why none of the women—or their vehicles—have been found."

Tucker cleared his throat. "I have to jump in here and say that there's no evidence supporting Walker's assertion." He tilted his head. "However, I think he makes a compelling argument."

"My cousin is a Texas Ranger," Walker added. "He's going back through these cases now, hoping to flush out new information that might help us. In the meantime, I believe we should focus on the crimes we can connect to Casanova. My sister's murder, Hayley's kidnapping, and the current threats."

"Hayley, I have a question." Jason reached down to stroke Connor's head. The German shepherd was sitting quietly next to his master. "Have you been back in Knoxville since the kidnapping? Before your mom died, I mean."

"No." Hayley tucked a strand of glossy hair behind her ear.

"Then it's possible your arrival in town triggered Casanova." Jason must've realized how that sounded because it quickly added, "Not that you're to blame for anything—"

She held up a hand to stop him, the scars that ended her career as an MP stark against her otherwise smooth skin. "You aren't saying anything I haven't already thought of. It's a fair deduction. I believe my presence in town caught Casanova's attention. On the day of Mom's funeral, someone broke into her house. The intruder laid out flowers and candles. He must've been watching the house for my arrival, because he called and taunted me. The voice was consistent with my recollections of Casanova."

Tucker leaned back in his chair, the police badge pinned to his chest shining in the fluorescent lights. "Would you be able to identify the owner of the voice if you heard it in a different context? For example, let's say Casanova ran into you in the bank lobby or on the street."

Hayley frowned. "I don't know. I have the sense he's manipulating his voice when he assumes the Casanova persona. Of course, that's just a feeling. I could be mistaken."

"Casanova left Hayley a threatening message and a bracelet." Walker pointed to photographs of each on the corkboard. "It took time, but we linked the jewelry to Julianna Clovers, a teacher at Knoxville High School. Evidence suggests Casanova murdered her. She was shot and a heart had been branded into her right shoulder."

"How did he get the bracelet?" Nathan asked.

"According to Julianna's friends, she lost it last week." Tucker got up and poured himself another cup of coffee. "Our best guess is that Casanova stole it. He also stalked her. Julianna complained to a couple of neighbors that she felt like someone was watching her. No one noticed anything unusual though."

Kyle drummed his fingers on the table. He was seated next to his cousin, Nathan. The family resemblance between the men was obvious. "Are we sure the man who kidnapped Hayley is the same one who killed Julianna? A teenager and a new mom are completely different kinds of victims. Also, Julianna wasn't kidnapped and taken somewhere else. She was murdered in her home."

"The murders are connected." Tucker sat back down at the table. "Forensics got back to me an hour ago. They compared the bullets used to kill both Lauren and Julianna." He met Walker's eyes. "They're a match."

A quiet hush filled the room. Walker had known the cases were connected, but having the evidence to support it made a difference. He breathed out.

"That doesn't mean we aren't looking at two different killers,"

Kyle argued. "Only that the same gun was used. Thomas—the man the former chief suspected of being Casanova—has a son, doesn't he?"

"Bobby Ray." Walker mulled over the argument his friend was making. As much as he hated to admit it, Kyle was on to something. "It's possible Thomas killed Lauren and kidnapped Hayley. Bobby Ray would've been eighteen. He could've uncovered what his dad was doing. Or Thomas told him. Then when Hayley came back to town, Bobby Ray decided to carry on the family legacy."

"It's possible, but I don't think we're looking at two different perpetrators." Hayley leaned forward on the table. "Casanova is adapting his methods. He's angry that I escaped and wants to get back at me. That much is clear from his letter. Hiding Julianna's body would defeat the point. Casanova wanted me to know she'd been murdered by him."

"It would also explain why he attempted to kill Walker," Jason added. "Casanova specifically mentioned Walker in the letter to Hayley, hoping it would bring the two of them together. He then tried to murder Walker in front of Hayley."

She nodded. "Exactly. He's toying with me." Hayley blew out a breath. "It's some kind of game to him. A competition between us." She pulled out her cell phone and laid it on the table. "I got another phone call from Casanova earlier this evening. Y'all should listen to it."

She hit play. Walker's stomach churned as he listened to the conversation again. It wasn't any easier to hear the second time around. Once it was done, no one spoke for a long time.

Then Jason breathed out. "You're right. This is a game to him." His mouth tightened, drawing the scar earned during combat down. "Casanova says he's been watching you for a long time. That indicates he knows about your career as an MP. You're not just the victim who got away. You're a cop too. It adds to the challenge."

Walker concurred with Jason's assessment. "He's definitely toying with Hayley, that's for sure."

"Sick." Logan's hands balled into fists. His teeth clenched together. "Could Bobby Ray Daniels be the killer? Hayley was held on his family's property. Bobby Ray had as much access as his father did to the shed."

"I suggested the same thing to Chief Garcia in our first meeting," Hayley said. "Bobby Ray has an extensive rap sheet. Assault, domestic violence, and drugs. He recently got out of prison."

Walker frowned and shook his head. "Bobby Ray has a temper but isn't terribly smart. I'm not sure he can plan a complicated murder." He pointed to the location of Knoxville High School. "Casanova's primary hunting ground is the high school. I suspect he's connected to it somehow. A former student, a teacher, an administrator. We need to look at everyone who was at the high school when Hayley went there and also when Julianna worked there."

"I can create that list." Kyle shifted his empty plate away. "And I'll do a background check on anyone of interest."

"I agree we shouldn't limit our suspect list to only Bobby Ray," Hayley said. "But given the evidence, he's a person of interest. I'd like to know where he was on the night Casanova broke into my mom's house and when Julianna was murdered."

"So would I." Tucker scraped a hand through his hair. "I went with Chief Garcia to speak to Bobby Ray. He refused to say a word without his lawyer. We dragged him into an interview at the station. The lawyer wouldn't allow him to answer questions. As of right now, we have no evidence linking him to any of the crimes and can't force him to talk to us."

"What if I went to speak to him?" Hayley arched her brows. "If Bobby Ray is Casanova, he might get a kick out of having me show up on his doorstep. Maybe he'll let something slip that will help."

"No." Walker didn't want her anywhere near the man. "That's like kicking a hornet nest."

She met his gaze. "Someone like Casanova is careful. Organized. He's working off a plan, and I'm certain he's already got his next victim picked out. Waiting for him to make the next move is a mistake. We need to rattle him." Hayley gave a predatory smile, determination hardening her gaze. "Kicking the hornet's nest is exactly what I want to do."

There was no way to talk her out of this. Once Hayley decided, that was it. Walker crossed his arms. "Then I'm going with you."

ELEVEN

The next morning, Hayley studied the GPS on her phone, doing her level best to ignore the knots twisting her insides. Talking to Bobby Ray was the right thing to do, but she hadn't calculated how difficult it would be to return to the location where she'd been held captive. Her palms were damp with perspiration. She willed herself to take a deep breath to control her jittery emotions. She didn't want to spiral into a panic attack.

"Slow down." Hayley studied the two-lane country road and then the map again. "The entrance to the property is coming up."

Walker hit the brakes, bringing the old ranch truck to a crawl. A short barbed-wire fence was tucked among the trees. Hayley didn't remember it being there before. Maybe the Daniels had fenced their property after she'd escaped from the shed. The land looked undeveloped and unused though. The woods were thick with brush, the ground covered in fallen branches and mountains of pine needles.

Hayley focused on the right side of the road, looking for any sign of a turnoff. A dented mailbox appeared. She pointed to it. "There."

The truck bounced over ruts and grooves in the dirt road leading to Bobby's Ray's house. Trees arched overhead, blocking out the sun, and branches scraped the side of the vehicle. Several wireless cameras had been strategically placed along the route. Walker pointed to one. "Looks like Bobby Ray is a fan of surveillance."

Hayley gripped the roll bar. "This is a rural location. The cameras could be for security." She glanced at Walker. "The other possibility is that Bobby Ray has something to hide and uses the cameras to ensure he isn't surprised by unannounced visitors."

"Like us."

He navigated a bend in the road and the house appeared. It was a one-story clapboard with a rusted metal roof. Unlike the surrounding property, the house showed signs of care. Someone had painted the trim a bright white and fresh boards on the porch indicated a recent repair. A rain bucket collected water from brand-new gutters.

Beyond the house was an old barn. It was also built in the same clapboard style of the house, but time had stripped away any sign of paint. It was a dull gray against the green and brown backdrop of the woods. Goats wandered the property, feeding on the grass.

A pit bull was chained nearby. He barked an unnecessary warning to his owners. Bobby Ray was already outside. He headed from the barn to the house, his long strides eating up the distance, a pitch fork slung over his shoulder. His expression was harsh and unwelcoming.

"You sure about this?" Walker murmured.

"Yes." Hayley snapped on her cop's armor. Emotional detachment wasn't easy, but it was necessary. She exited the vehicle. Cold air whipped her cheeks as she came around the front of the truck.

Bobby Ray stumbled. He quickly recovered, his gaze shooting to Walker who'd joined Hayley in the grass. Her ex stayed back a pace. Close enough to protect her if necessary, but far enough away as to not be threatening to Bobby Ray.

The bully Hayley had known in high school looked different. Prison and a life of crime had aged him. His hair was turning prematurely gray, and deep grooves lined the area under his eyes. His nose was crooked, as if it'd been broken a time or two. Barrel-chested and stocky, he'd gained weight around his midsection. He was dressed in beat-up blue jeans, filthy work boots, and a jacket. Bobby Ray was only in his early thirties, but appeared a decade older.

He stopped a short distance away from her. The hostility melted from his expression, replaced by a weariness. A flash of something akin to guilt creased his features before disappearing. "What are you doing here?"

"I came to talk." She kept her tone and expression polite. Bobby Ray had a criminal record, but that didn't make him a killer. Hayley needed to tread lightly when questioning him. "Casanova contacted me."

"I'm aware." His mouth hardened. "The police came to question me. I'll tell them what I told you. I have nothing to say."

"Not even if it means clearing your father's name?"

Bobby Ray stiffened, and then he glowered at her. "You don't care a fig about my father's name."

"That's not true. I never accused your dad of being Casanova. The police made that connection, and it's come to my attention that the old police chief was corrupt. Based on the recent threats made toward me, I believe he made a mistake." Hayley held his gaze. "I intend to find Casanova and put him in jail. For good."

He snorted and pointed a dirty fingernail in her direction. "I'm not a fool, Hayley. You're gonna pin this on me." His gaze drifted to Walker, and a sneer curled the corner of his mouth. "If you wanted to give me a fair shot, you wouldn't have brought Montgomery with you."

Hayley glanced over her shoulder at Walker, but his gaze was locked on Bobby Ray. Clearly the old grudge from high school was still ongoing.

Bobby Ray had been one of the bullies picking on a freshman, and in the subsequent fight, Walker had broken Bobby Ray's nose. The hostility hadn't ended there. Bobby Ray attempted to goad

Walker into a rematch by threatening him with a knife. The only thing he accomplished was losing yet another fight and being permanently suspended from high school. Bobby Ray's arrest record picked up after that as he turned to a life of crime. Things only got worse after his father was accused of being Casanova. Bobby Ray got deep into drugs. He'd been her mother's dealer for a time, a fact Hayley didn't like to think about.

The tension between Walker and Bobby Ray was thicker than the storm clouds hovering on the horizon. A low rumble of thunder warned that rain wasn't far away. Hayley shivered as an icy wind slipped down her jacket collar. The memory of Casanova's phone call flashed in her mind. The killer had tried to hide it, but there had been anger in his voice when speaking about Walker.

"I'm not interested in pinning this on anyone, Bobby Ray." Hayley took a step in his direction, drawing his attention away from Walker and back toward her. "I'm after the truth. Same as you. Help me find it."

"How?"

"You can start by answering some questions. For starters, where were you on Wednesday night?" That was the day of her mom's funeral. Casanova had left roses and his first message for her that evening.

Silence dragged out as Bobby Ray stared at the ground. Hayley could tell he was considering his options. Tension poured off his muscles, and he gripped the pitchfork tightly enough to turn his knuckles white. She sensed he was one breath away from telling them to get off his property.

Then Bobby Ray sighed, long and low. "My answer won't help. I was here." He hiked the pitch fork higher on his shoulder. "Believe it or not, I'm tired of prison and the constant stress that comes with it. I'm done. All I want is to live quietly and be left alone."

Hayley couldn't tell if he was lying. Bobby Ray sounded genuine, but he'd been manipulative in high school. She kept her hands at her sides, her stance casual. "Can anyone confirm that?"

"My mother." He smirked. "But I doubt anyone will believe her. Moms lie for their kids all the time, don't they?"

He had a point. Hayley shifted tactics. "When did you find out I'd been held on your property?"

"After you escaped, just like everyone else." He waved a hand toward the forest. "It's not like we go hiking back there. My dad didn't even remember that shed was there until the police came pounding on our door with a search warrant." Bobby Ray glowered. "They tore our house apart, but never found evidence linking my dad to the crime. Of course, that didn't stop everyone in town from making assumptions. It ruined my dad's business. He closed the convenience store and..."

Thomas eventually committed suicide. As much as Hayley tried to keep her emotions in check, she couldn't help but have sympathy for Bobby Ray. His father had been suspected of a horrific crime and there'd been no way to prove his innocence. It must've been terrible for the family.

The screen door on the house creaked. A woman stepped out onto the porch. Her gray hair was tied back into a low ponytail and a washed-out apron covered her thin dress. Bobby Ray's mother. Like her son, Regina Daniels had aged drastically. Her complexion was ghostly pale, her face crisscrossed with lines. Regina's gaze swept across her son and then Hayley before landing on Walker.

She scowled, deep creases forming around her eyes. "What are you doing here?"

Her words were meant for Walker, but Hayley answered, "We're speaking with Bobby Ray."

"He's got nothing to say." Regina marched off the porch, her shoes crunching the leaves scattered in the yard with the force of her steps. She hooked a hand around Bobby Ray's arm and tugged him toward the house. "We don't know anything. Just leave us alone."

"Mrs. Daniels—"

She let go of her son and whirled around. "No."

The hostility in that one word stopped Hayley cold.

Regina sucked in a breath. "I'm sorry for what happened to you, but no one here is responsible for it. My job is to protect my son. Now, get off my land. You're trespassing."

With those final words, she grabbed Bobby Ray's arm. Together they went inside the house. The screen door slammed shut behind them.

Hayley let go of the breath she was holding, condensation forming in front of her face. She shared a glance with Walker before getting back into the truck. He fired up the engine and did a three-point turn. Movement in a window next to the door drew Hayley's attention. She glanced in the side-view mirror.

Bobby Ray watched them go. His expression was unreadable. Not sadness, or worry... more like menace. Direct at her? Or Walker?

As if he could sense her watching him, Bobby Ray lifted a hand to wave goodbye.

It sent a chill straight through Hayley.

TWELVE

Half an hour later, Hayley balanced a tray of coffees on her lap as Walker turned into the parking lot of Knoxville High School. Her mind hadn't stopped whirling since leaving Bobby Ray's place. The man was off-putting, but the interest in clearing his dad's name appeared genuine. She wasn't sure what to make of it.

Walker pulled into an empty spot and killed the engine. His hand tightened on the steering wheel. "Chris's background check came back clean, but just because he's never been arrested, doesn't mean he's innocent. We can't clear anyone off the suspect list yet."

"I know, but Bobby Ray is at the top. We need more information about him. Since Chris and Bobby Ray were once friends, but aren't anymore, he's our best option."

"I agree, but you don't have to question him by yourself."

"Chris is more likely to open up if you aren't there." Hayley undid her seat belt and tossed him an effortless smile. "I appreciate the backup, but the Army trained me well. I know how to handle myself. Talking to Chris in the high school parking lot is low risk. Even if he's Casanova, he won't attack me here."

Walker glowered. "I wouldn't be so sure. Someone took potshots at us the other day."

Hayley waved a finger. "Nuh-uh. Not us. You." She opened the truck door and exited, careful to keep the coffees level. "Which reminds me. Try not to get shot while I'm gone."

"Funny." He rolled his eyes. "Real funny."

Hayley chuckled. She shut the passenger-side door and shivered as the warmth trapped in her coat from the truck's heaters was replaced by frigid air. She hunched her shoulders against the wind. Storm clouds lingered in the distance but hadn't moved over the town yet.

Chris was standing near his golf cart in a small alcove. He rubbed his hands together before shoving them in his pockets. Hayley felt a pang of sympathy for him. On pretty days, being outside would be a blessing. But in this weather, it was miserable.

He spotted her coming toward him and smiled. "Hey there."

"Hey." She returned his friendly greeting. Chris stepped from the alcove, but Hayley waved him back. She lifted the coffees in her hand. "I brought something to warm you up. It's freezing today."

"Sure is. Coldest week of the year, according to the weatherman. We don't get snow, but there's something about a Texas winter that bites."

"It's a damp cold. Shoots straight to your bones." She ducked inside the alcove. The three brick walls provided protection from the wind, and Hayley was instantly warmer. She handed Chris a take-away mug. "I didn't know how you like your coffee. It's black, but I've got sugar and creamer in my pockets."

"Black is great." He sipped the drink and sighed. "Just what I needed. Thanks."

"You're welcome." She gestured to the yellow ribbons tied around the trees on the school grounds. "Are those for Julianna?"

"Yeah." Chris propped a shoulder against the brick, his expression instantly falling and his mood darkening. "I can't believe someone killed her. It's awful. She was..." Tears shimmered in his eyes. Chris swallowed twice as if to clear a lump from his throat and then continued, "Julianna was kind to everyone. My job is somewhat invisible, you know. Some teachers and staff ignore me like I'm nothing. Not Julianna. She always stopped to say hello to me every morning. Remembered to ask about my cat, Charlie, and discuss the latest episode of a television show we both liked."

His grief was palpable. Hayley's chest tightened in response. An image of Sophia flashed in her mind and the sadness deepened. Julianna's little girl wouldn't remember her mom. It was a tragedy from every angle.

"What happened is horrible." Hayley tilted her head. If Chris spoke to Julianna so often, why hadn't he recognized her bracelet? A sliver of doubt worked its way through her previous convictions. "I didn't realize you and Julianna were close."

"I wouldn't call us close, but she was kind to me. Few people are, you know." Chris turned to face her, keeping his back to the brick. "I'm still as socially awkward as I was in high school. Friendships don't come easily." His brow creased. "Are the rumors going around town true? Was Julianna killed by Casanova?"

"No one is certain. The police are investigating."

"Mrs. Haverstein told me it was Julianna's bracelet in the picture you had. Then you and Walker found Julianna's body." Chris's mouth hardened. "What's going on, Hayley? Seriously. Are you in some kind of trouble?"

"I don't know." She weighed how much to share but decided it didn't matter. Leaks in any police department were difficult to control, and in a town like Knoxville, it was a given. Besides, if Chris was Casanova, he already knew everything anyway. "I've been receiving threats from someone claiming to be Casanova. I'm not sure if it's the same man as the one who kidnapped me or someone different."

"Why would anyone pretend to be Casanova..." His eyes

widened with sudden understanding. "Bobby Ray."

He caught on quick. Chris might be socially awkward, but he was smart. Once again, that niggle of doubt tugged at her. She stared at the man tucked in the alcove alongside her. He wore a thick jacket that strained to stay closed around his bulky form. Chris had always been strong and big, even back in high school. She tried to remember what Casanova had looked like, but her recollections were hazy. He'd kept her drugged in the shed.

When she and Lauren had first been carjacked though... Casanova had been a big guy. Nearly too big for the back seat of her car.

But Chris had never made her uncomfortable or pressed an advantage. Even now, he positioned his body away from her to provide as much space in the alcove between them as possible. Would Casanova do that?

No. He wouldn't.

She breathed and mentally gave herself a shake. Working this case, keeping some kind of neutral perspective, was much harder than Hayley wanted it to be. She took a long sip of her coffee. "I don't want to point fingers, but it crossed my mind that Bobby Ray could be involved."

"I wouldn't put it past him. He was furious the police kept questioning his dad. Bobby Ray believes Thomas committed suicide because of the case." He squinted. "He's the kind who'd want revenge."

"Do you think Thomas was Casanova?"

"I don't know." Chris's gaze drifted over the parking lot. "Thomas didn't show any sign of aggression when I was around, but people can be good at hiding the worst parts of themselves. I can tell you he was a serial cheater, and that caused some friction between him and Bobby Ray." He took a drink of his coffee. "There's something you should know. Bobby Ray isn't the only one who might want revenge. Aaron Parker and Bobby Ray were half-brothers."

Hayley's mouth dropped. Aaron Parker was another bully who ran in the same crowd with Bobby Ray. "I had no idea."

"Most people didn't. They kept it hush-hush, for the most part. Thomas had quite a few kids outside of his marriage. Bobby Ray used to say he wouldn't be surprised if some stranger came knocking on his door to say they were brothers. It was a joke, but I could tell it bothered him."

"Yet he was close to Aaron."

"Yeah, but Aaron and Bobby Ray had the same mentality. A sense of cruelty that ran deep."

"Did Aaron and his dad spend time together?"

"Some. Thomas didn't officially claim him out of respect for his wife, but he used to do things for Aaron here and there. Give money if he needed it. One time, he bailed him out of jail." Chris absently played with his goatee. "Last I heard, Aaron had disappeared to Houston and took up with some gang. I wouldn't be surprised if he was dead, but if he isn't..."

"Maybe he's involved." Hayley's mind whirled with the new information. "You've given me a lot to think about."

Chris turned and met her gaze. "Be careful, Hayley. Guys like Bobby Ray and Aaron are cold-blooded. If either of them has taken over for their dad, they won't stop until they've gotten revenge."

She nodded. "Understood." Hayley stepped out of the alcove but then turned. "Do you think it's possible either Bobby Ray or Aaron is Casanova? Could either of them be the one who kidnapped me the first time?"

He was quiet for a long moment. Then he sighed, long and heavy, his shoulders dropping as if realizing just the type of men he'd once been friends with. "Yes, Hayley. Either of them could be Casanova."

"Would Thomas have protected them by lying to the police or pretending to be Casanova to keep law enforcement from suspecting either of his sons?"

"Without a doubt."

THIRTEEN

Walker pulled into the parking lot of Nelson's Diner. Thunder rumbled as he got out of the truck and circled to the passenger side. He opened the door and offered Hayley a hand. She slipped her fingers into his. They were ice cold, despite the truck's heater running on full blast during the car ride over. Concern shot through Walker. Hayley was extremely good at compartmentalizing her feelings, but her body betrayed her, if a person knew how to read the signs.

The conversation with Chris had upset her. Hayley had given him a rundown and then fallen silent. Walker had the sense she was mulling things over and let her be. She'd always needed time to organize her observations.

Walker tugged her closer as they crossed the parking lot. His gaze never stopped scanning their immediate surroundings, searching for a possible sniper. Every minute they spent off the ranch was potentially dangerous. Not that the gorgeous woman at his side wasn't capable of taking care of herself. She was former military. Still, Walker's protective instincts were in high gear. He couldn't change that fact any more than he could stop breathing.

The scents of warm pastries and fresh fries enveloped Walker the moment he followed Hayley into the diner. His stomach rumbled. First things first, food. Then discuss the recent developments in the case. Everything was easier with a full belly.

Harriet, the owner, greeted them with a broad smile that smushed her cheeks. Her steel gray hair was formed into tight curls that bounced as she came around the counter to give them both a hug. First Walker and then Hayley.

"I'm so glad y'all came in to visit." Harriet pulled back and patted Hayley's cheek. "The town's been buzzing about what happened to you the other night. I'm so glad you're okay, sweetie."

"Thanks. It's been... tough." Shadows crossed Hayley's expression before her mouth lifted in a slight smile. "Do you have any cherry cobbler? I could use some after a plate of your fabulous meatloaf."

Harriet beamed. "I've got more than just cherry cobbler and meatloaf. Leave everything to me. I'll fill your belly up so much, you'll have to roll out of here." She turned to Walker and winked. "I've got a fresh lemon meringue for you."

He grinned. "I knew you wouldn't let me down."

Harriet laughed. She snagged some silverware and a couple of placemats before escorting them to a booth in the rear. Walker raised his hand to wave to Nelson, visible in the kitchen through a cutout behind the counter. The older man waved a spatula in greeting. Waitresses moved from table to table, handling the lunch rush. Harriet took their orders.

Hayley tossed a straw into her water glass and then shredded the wrapper. It looked like she had something to say but wasn't sure how to phrase it. Then she balled the torn paper. "I keep turning over everything Chris said and comparing it to the memories of Casanova's attack on me, trying to determine which man was hunched in my back seat."

"And?"

"I can't come to a clear conclusion. I remember more about Lauren than I do about the attacker." She rubbed her forehead. "Why didn't I pay more attention?"

"Hey, don't beat yourself up. It was a terrifying situation, and you were focused on trying to save Lauren's life." He covered her hand with his. "You did the best you could."

She breathed out and dropped her other hand from her forehead. "Right. The thing to do now is focus on the information we have. Chris made it clear he believe Bobby Ray could be involved. Trouble is, Bobby Ray seemed genuinely interested in clearing his father's name. I'm not sure he was telling the truth about his alibi though. It would've helped to have his mom confirm it."

Walker shrugged. "Not necessarily. She's the type to lie if it means protecting her son."

"True. Did Kyle send you the background info on Aaron?"

"Yeah." He pulled it up on his phone. "The guy has a rap sheet longer than my arm. Been arrested a bunch, but has avoided doing long stints in prison." He paused. "That seems to be a theme I keep running up against. How are these people being arrested for theft and attempted murder, and then not actually going to jail?"

"Plea deals. It's expensive to conduct a trial." Hayley took the phone and scrolled through Aaron's criminal record. "Last known address is in Houston. What are the chances we'll actually find him there?"

"Not high, but I'll ask my cousin, Ryker, to check." Walker was quiet for a long moment. "You know, Bobby Ray and Aaron might not be involved. If what Chris said is true, and Thomas had several children outside of his marriage, any of them could've had access to the Daniels property."

"I know." Hayley tipped her head. "We need to be careful here. I don't think it's a good idea to limit our viewpoint to members of the Daniels family. Thomas could've been telling the truth about the shed. It was on a wooded area of the property that was unused.

Anyone could've learned about it and accessed it without the Daniels family knowing."

Walker nodded. "Like Chris. He was Bobby Ray's friend, had been to the house several times. He could've told you this information about the Daniels family to muddy the waters."

"I hate to admit it, but you're right. Still, Chris has never once made me feel uncomfortable. It's a gut feeling, which can't be relied on, but still... I don't think he's involved."

Walker respected her opinion. Gut feelings weren't proof, but listening to them had saved his life more than once. He wouldn't take Chris off the suspect list, but the security guard dropped to the bottom. They could always reevaluate if new evidence came up. "Speaking of gut feelings, there's something I've been meaning to ask you. What's the issue between you and Richard Westbrook?"

Her brows arched. "Our former-math-teacher-turned-principal?"

"Yeah. Chris doesn't make you uncomfortable, but Westbrook did. Any reason why?"

"No. I just don't like him. Never did. Mr. Westbrook has this false sense about him." Her brows creased, and a frown drew the corners of her mouth down. "I can't explain it any better than that. It's just a feeling I get from him. Insincere."

Again, her observation supported his own. Walker made a mental note to do a background check on Richard. It was a long shot that he was Casanova—the man had been a long-standing member of the community—but Walker wouldn't leave any stone unturned.

"Here we are." Harriet appeared and plopped two steaming bowls on the table, filled to the brim with soup. "A little something to warm you up on a cold day. On the house." She smiled. "Your meat-loaf specials will be out in a jiffy."

They each thanked her and she bustled off.

Hayley bowed her head for a moment in prayer before picking up her spoon. She twirled it in the soup. "It's veggie. Yummy." She lifted a taste to her mouth and closed her eyes in bliss. "So good. I've missed Harriet's cooking."

They ate and, by some silent agreement, switched topics away from the case. Walker was curious about Hayley's life in North Carolina. He peppered her with questions. She told him several funny stories about her colleagues and a few cases. The soup was replaced by the main course and then dessert. Time slipped by as the conversation kept flowing. Walker told Hayley about the bombing, his subsequent leg injury, and the return home in more detail. He entertained her with amusing stories about his stubborn dad.

Then it was Hayley's turn to ask questions about his friends. The Special Forces, as she'd taken to calling them, adopting Chief Garcia's nickname. Walker had given her an overview before, but now he explained in full the cases they'd been embroiled in and how the group faced each one.

When he was finished, she sat back in the booth. "Wow. I have a few thoughts." Hayley held up a finger. "One, I'm glad you have such an amazing group of people to watch your back. Two, who knew so much crime happened in tiny Knoxville? And three..." She shook her head. "I can't believe they all met their wives while saving them from dangerous situations. What a story to tell your grandkids, huh?"

Walker chuckled. "True. Funnily enough, none of the guys were interested in relationships beforehand either. It just happened." He pushed aside his empty dessert plate. "Now, they're talking kids. Kyle and Sierra have Daniel, but want more children. Jason and Addison are expecting their first. Tucker and Leah are in the process of adoption. I don't think Cassie and Nathan will wait much longer, although they haven't said much. Pretty soon, there's going to be a group of ankle biters running around at our barbecues."

Hayley twirled the straw in her water glass. "And what about you? Don't you still want to get married and have children?"

"I don't know. Things have changed." He paused. Hayley was his ex, but more than that, she'd been his best friend. She was one of the few people who'd known him before everything in his life was torn apart. If anyone would understand his thoughts, it would be her. "I've changed. Marriage and kids require a hopefulness about life that I don't have anymore. Lauren's death and my time in the SEALs taught me that things can be taken away just like that." Walker snapped his fingers. "It's hard to let go of that fear."

"Prayer helps." Hayley reached across the table and took his hand. "Not that I'm someone who should give advice about this subject. I haven't had luck in the dating department. But, Walker, you're amazing. I'd hate for you to miss out on marriage and kids because of the awful things you've experienced. The good in this world far outweighs the bad."

The tattoo on her wrist was visible, and Walker ran his thumb over it. He'd lost some of his faith along the way. "Do you really believe that? The good outweighs the bad?"

"With all my heart." Her tone was tender. "It's difficult to see sometimes. I'll admit that. But God brings goodness into our lives even in the darkest of times. Like now. He brought you and me together to help each other through this. No one would understand what I'm going through the way you do." She met his gaze. "Don't get me wrong. It would be better if Casanova was locked up or dead. But if I have to face these challenges, then I'm glad to be doing them with you."

His breath hitched. The moment drew out as Walker noticed every place their skin touched. The smooth silkiness of Hayley's palm, the delicate structure of her bones. The way she looked at him... it was hard to describe. Not just with gratitude, or friendship, or even longing.

Hayley saw who he truly was. The doubts, the fears, and the greatness. She accepted him wholeheartedly while pushing him gently in a direction necessary for growth. Walker had forgotten how intoxicating that was.

The calluses developed around his heart for protection cracked.

He wanted them to. He was tired of feeling alone. Maybe it was time for a mindset shift. Walker committed to seeing things in a new way.

I'm opening my heart, Lord. I'm turning to you. Please, help me.

Walker threaded his fingers through Hayley's. "You're right. If we have to go through this, then I'm glad to be doing it with you." He gently squeezed her hand. "I've missed you, Hails."

Her beautiful eyes shimmered with sudden tears. "I've missed you too."

Walker released her hand long enough to come around to her side of the booth. He squeezed into the seat and then pulled her into his arms. "Shoot, I didn't mean to make you cry." He cupped her face and wiped away the tears. "You almost never cry."

"I know. What's wrong with me?" She sounded exacerbated. Hayley grabbed a napkin and swiped at her face. "That's twice in two days."

He chuckled and wrapped an arm around her shoulders. "It's been an emotional few days."

"Yeah, it has." Hayley leaned on his chest. "Will you judge me if I order more cherry cobbler and ice cream?"

He burst out laughing. "Not even a little. In fact, another slice of lemon meringue might go down nicely." He waved to Harriet, pointed to the empty plates, and followed it up with a two. She nodded, understanding immediately that they wanted more dessert. "We can even take some cherry cobbler home—"

His phone beeped. Walker shifted in the booth to pull it out of his pocket. His heart stopped as he read the text message from Tucker. "A local woman is missing. Kelly Fraser. She's a brunette and works at the Knoxville library." Hayley sat up to face him and Walker continued reading, "Tucker is at her home. There's sign of a struggle, but no sign of where Kelly is."

"When was she last seen?"

He kept reading. "Last night. Lives alone. A neighbor saw her return from work at six, but she didn't move her car the next morning.

The library reported her missing when she didn't show up to work this morning. The reappearance of Casanova has been all over the news and they were concerned for Kelly's welfare."

Hayley closed her eyes for a moment before snapping them open. "Can we go to her house? I'd like to see the crime scene, if possible."

"It's worth a shot. Tucker's on site. He might let you walk through." Walker stood and threw enough cash on the table to cover the bill, including the extra desserts that they wouldn't eat now. The food in his stomach congealed into a lump as adrenaline shot through his veins. He couldn't imagine putting another bite in his mouth.

Hayley was rising out of the booth when her cell phone rang. She stiffened for half a heartbeat before pulling it from her pocket. The number on her screen was local but unfamiliar. Different from the other day. Still, Walker knew instantly who was calling. Kyle had traced the numbers Casanova had previous called from to burner phones. He used a different one every time.

Walker's jaw clenched. "It's him. Casanova."

Hayley nodded. Her expression hardened into an unreadable mask. Her cop face. A protective measure to shield her emotions and provide some distance from what was about to happen. Walker didn't blame her for it. He used the method many times while on deployment or carrying out a mission. Emotions could get a person killed. He snapped his own armor into place.

Then Hayley answered the phone.

FOURTEEN

"Hello, sweetheart."

The soft, Southern drawl mixed with the term of endearment roiled Hayley's insides. She gripped the cell phone tighter, pressing the device against her ear until it hurt. Putting the call on speaker for Walker to listen in wasn't an option. They were still inside the diner. Other patrons might overhear.

Instead, Hayley quickly walked to an alcove near the kitchen for privacy. Walker followed without question. Once inside the quieter space, she put the call on speaker. "Did you kidnap Kelly?"

"Of course. Kelly, say hello to Hayley for me."

A woman's scream came over the line. It was bloodcurdling. Terrified. Despite her best effort to maintain emotional distance, that guttural cry reached right inside Hayley's chest and stole her breath. The brand on her shoulder burned.

"Stop!" Hayley yelled the command, unable to keep control. "Stop hurting her!"

The scream cut off.

Hayley's knees went weak. Walker wrapped an arm around her

waist, and she leaned into his strong form. He was the only thing grounding her.

"Don't hurt her." Hayley barely recognized her own voice. It was hollow. Wrung out. "What do you want?"

"For you to do exactly as I say."

She didn't have a choice. Hayley would do anything to keep Casanova's attention on her and not on Kelly. "Done. In fact, we can make a trade. Me for Kelly. Tell me where to meet you."

Walker stiffened.

Hayley held up a finger to keep him from speaking a word. This was her bargain to make, and she'd do what was necessary to save Kelly's life. Hayley had intimate knowledge of the terror the poor woman was going through at the moment.

"An intriguing offer, sweetheart." Casanova hummed. "One I'll have to think about. In the meantime, let's continue playing the game, shall we? I've left a gift for you outside the diner. It's on the back fence. Sorry I can't deliver it myself, but I had to get back to Kelly."

Hayley's gaze met Walker's as an icy river of shock washed over her. Casanova had been here. At the diner while they were eating. Neither of them had seen or noticed anything unusual. "What kind of gift?"

"A clue. Figure it out in time and you can save Kelly's life." His tone was toying. Casanova was enjoying this. He controlled her, just as he'd done when she was captive and at his mercy. "This time, Hayley, play by the rules, or I'll get mad. And we both know what happens when I get mad."

"The police are already involved. How do you think I knew Kelly was missing?"

"Don't be stupid." His words were as sharp as blades. "It doesn't suit you. I don't want you sharing the clues with the police or using them to chase down leads. This is between you and me."

And Walker. She added that last bit mentally. With Kelly at Casanova's mercy, she wouldn't do anything to anger him further.

"Okay, I won't involve the police." Hayley gripped the phone hard enough to make her fingers ache. "Don't hurt Kelly."

"Don't make me. Tick tock, sweetheart. You don't have much time."

He hung up.

Hayley lowered the phone and took a deep breath to clear the adrenaline narrowing her vision. She hurried out of the alcove and across the diner. Walker was right behind her.

Please, God, help me be strong. Give me the wisdom and ability to save Kelly.

The prayer eased her inner turmoil but didn't erase the urgency of her steps as she shoved the main door to the diner open. Cold air smacked her cheeks. Rain pattered against her bare head, soaking her hair. She hadn't bothered to retrieve her coat from the booth. Goose bumps broke out across her skin.

Hayley took several seconds to assess the parking lot. Only a few patrons were left inside, the diner clearing out after the lunch rush. She put a hand up to stop Walker from stepping over the threshold. Her attention swept across the building, the nearby trees, and the gas station down the road. No sign of a sniper.

Walker stepped into the rain. "Don't worry about me, Hayley. I know how to handle myself."

She couldn't help it. The idea of Walker being injured—or worse, killed—it was more than she could process at the moment. Hayley didn't want to think too hard about how deep her feelings were for the handsome SEAL. That was a road leading straight to trouble, and she had enough problems on her plate at the moment. She swiped a hand over her lashes to clear them of water droplets. "Let's go. Casanova said the note was on the back fence."

She ran around the side of the building at a fast clip, keeping her gaze alert and her ears pricked for any sound beyond the rainfall. Casanova wasn't one to play fair. He could be leading them straight into a trap.

The back fence came into view. A heart charm wrapped around a rose leaned against a wooden post next to an envelope with her name typed on it.

She paused long enough to take several photographs. Recording evidence was second nature. Then Hayley pinched the corner of the envelope with her nails. "Let's get inside."

Out here, they were too exposed. Too vulnerable. Maybe it was her imagination, but she sensed eyes on them. The hair on the back of her neck stood on end. From the expression on Walker's face, he felt it too. His focus never stopped moving. His gaze constantly shifted, watching for any sign of danger.

Walker placed a hand on the small of her back. "This way."

He led her to a door in the rear and pounded on it. A second later, it was opened by Nelson. He was dressed in a stained apron, and a chef's hat covered his bald head. In one hand, he held a shotgun. His expression was grim as he waved them inside. "Thank goodness you two are okay. Harriet saw you hurry out and was worried there was trouble."

The door slammed shut behind Walker.

Despite the trouble facing them, a wave of affection sliced through Hayley as she registered the worry lurking in Nelson's eyes. The older man was something akin to a grandfather to her. She hugged him quickly. "Thank you."

Nelson cleared his throat as if surprised by a sudden rush of emotion. "I don't like the idea of you being in trouble." He glanced at Walker. "What happened?"

While Walker gave a rundown of Casanova's phone call, Hayley found a set of plastic gloves in the kitchen and tugged them on. Probably foolish to waste the time. Casanova wouldn't handle the envelope or the note inside without gloves of his own, but habits were hard to break. Hayley's law enforcement training was embedded.

Once again, the flap on the envelope wasn't sealed. She lifted it. A necklace slid out onto the stainless-steel counter. It was gold, dainty, and had two charms. One was a cross. The other was the letter K.

Walker came up next to her. He'd also pulled on a set of gloves. He lifted the necklace. "The K is probably for Kelly. I'll send a photograph of this to Tucker. I'm sure he'll confirm Kelly was wearing this when she was kidnapped."

Hayley nodded initially and then halted. "Wait." She wouldn't completely abide by Casanova's command, but she also wouldn't risk Kelly's life. "Tucker needs to keep everything we give him under wraps. Only he and Chief Garcia can know about it. In a town this size, even with the best police department, there are leaks. We can't take a chance that someone will say something to the wrong person."

"Agreed."

The kitchen door swung open and Harriet rushed in, a worried look on her face. She was intercepted by her husband, who spoke to her in hushed tones. Hayley ignored the couple and turned her attention to the note. It was rain spattered.

She read the typewritten message out loud. "The murdered do haunt their murderers. I believe – I know that ghosts have wandered the earth. Be with me always – take any form – drive me mad."

Walker's brow furrowed. "What kind of clue is that?"

"I don't know." Hayley reached for her phone and quickly typed the message into the search bar. "It's a quote from a book. *Wuthering Heights*. I've never read it." She glanced at Walker. "Have you?"

He shook his head.

"I have." Harriet came closer. She twisted a dishcloth in her wrinkled hands. "The book is about a man named Heathcliff who becomes obsessed with vengeance when his supposed soulmate marries someone else." Her gaze skirted back and forth between Walker and Hayley. "I'm not sure what clue Casanova is providing, but he's definitely sending you a message."

The wisdom of Harriet's observation sunk into Hayley. Vengeance. Obsession. She inhaled sharply. "Casanova was in love with me, but I didn't feel the same way." She mulled over the new information. "That's why he's fixated on you, Walker. It's not Lauren's murder or the fact that you were looking for him. He can't stand that you're the man I fell in love with."

Fell in love. Present tense. Hayley caught the meaning of her words after they left her mouth, but it was too late to snatch them back. Did she love Walker? Maybe. Hayley wasn't sure she'd ever fallen out of love with him. But right now wasn't the time to think about it.

If Walker caught her faux pas, he didn't let on. His attention was still on the note. "Okay, even if all of that is true, how does this note help us find Kelly?"

Hayley went back through the information she had. "Didn't Tucker say that Kelly worked at Knoxville library? *Wuthering Heights* is a classic. They must have a copy."

"You think he put another clue inside the book?"

She snatched up the note and the necklace. "There's only one way to find out."

FIFTEEN

"He's sending us on a wild goose chase." Walker breezed through a yellow light and took a turn toward the center of town. The library was nestled between a hairdresser and a coffee shop. At this hour of the afternoon, it would be full of students. Mostly high school, but some junior high kids, and possibly even grade schoolers. The Knoxville library was a popular—and safe—hangout for youngsters. Walker couldn't help wondering if that's what Casanova was counting on. "Or he's leading us into a trap."

"I agree, but we have little choice." Hayley drummed her fingers against the door handle. "Do you think Bobby Ray had Kelly on his property while we were there? He came out of the barn when we arrived."

Walker had considered it. "It's possible. To think we were that close to Kelly..." He hit the steering wheel with the heel of his hand. "We're getting nowhere fast on this."

With a woman's life hanging in the balance, every second felt like sand slipping through his fingers. Walker was used to handling high-stress situations. He'd been deployed many times. Faced combat and been shot at. But this was pushing him to his limits.

He'd failed to protect his sister. Would he fail Kelly? And Hayley?

As if she'd read his thoughts, Hayley placed a hand on his shoulder. "Lord, we ask that You guide our movements. Use us as instruments to do Your will. We also pray for Kelly. In this time of pain and hurt, we ask that You are with her. Provide her comfort. Ease her suffering. Amen."

"Amen." Walker took her hand in his before brushing a kiss across her knuckles. Hayley's prayer served as a reminder that ultimately God was in charge. Walker could do his best—and he would—but he was only human. There were limitations to what he controlled. "You're right, Hails. Prayer helps."

The library appeared on the right-hand side. Walker pulled into the parking lot. He parked as close to the main doors as possible. The rain had quieted to a drizzle. Hayley was already scanning the tops of buildings, searching for any sign of a sniper. Her sharp-eyed gaze swept the parking lot too.

Walker did the same. "Looks clear to me."

"Same. Let's go."

They exited the vehicle and hurried inside. The door swished closed behind them. Several librarians sat behind a long rectangular desk. The air smelled of old books. A group of teens were gathered around a circular table, doing some kind of group project. Computers lined the far wall, available for use by patrons. The children's section was in the rear. A sign on the front counter announced Story Time was taking place.

Walker resisted the urge to shout at everyone to go home. His nerves were jittery and his skin crawling with unresolved tension. He muttered another prayer. Maybe it wasn't right for Walker to turn to the Lord now when he'd been lost in the faith department, but the petitions weren't for him. It was for the innocent people in the library. For Hayley. For Kelly.

The door opened behind him. Walker turned as Richard Westbrook entered the building. The principal of Knoxville High was dressed in slacks and a button-down. He shook rain drops off his jacket. His thinning hair was even more sparse when damp.

Hayley, who'd been asking the librarian about *Wuthering Heights* at the front desk, abandoned the task and joined Walker. "What's he doing here?" she whispered.

It was a good question. Had Richard followed them? Then again, he could be here for a completely benign reason. They were in a public library after all. Walker plastered a friendly smile on his face. "Principal Westbrook. Hi."

The principal smiled in greeting, although it didn't quite reach his eyes. "Hey, Walker." He glanced at Hayley and nodded. "Hayley. What a pleasure running into you again. Twice in one week." Richard shrugged out of his jacket. "The weather is just awful today. We're supposed to get more rain tomorrow, can you believe it?"

"It's winter weather, for sure. Do you come to the library often?"

"No. I'm picking up my daughter." He craned his neck to see around Walker. "She's working on a group project with her classmates."

Walker rocked back on his heels. Richard's explanation for being at the library was reasonable. It could simply be a coincidence they ran into each other, but Walker couldn't shake the sense that it was more. He decided to poke Richard and see what kind of reaction followed. "I'm sorry about Julianna."

Richard's expression fell. "Oh, yes. It's tragic." His gaze locked on Hayley. "I heard you found her body. I can't imagine how terrible that must've been for you."

It took everything inside Walker to keep his stance casual and his muscles relaxed. Richard was focused on Hayley in a way that didn't feel normal. Then again, he'd felt the same about Bobby Ray. Was he completely losing his mind? Seeing potential killers around every corner?

Hayley tilted her head, her dark hair falling over her forehead. "Were you close to Julianna?"

"No. Not particularly. Of course, I care about all the faculty and staff at the high school, but it's difficult to get to know each one on a close and personal basis. The students are devastated by the loss though. They adored her." His brow crinkled. "Do you know if the police have any leads on who murdered her? There are rumors going around town that Casanova had something to do with it. The police chief was interviewed by a reporter last night, but he's not saying much."

Chief Garcia was smart. He wouldn't tell the public anything unless he was certain about it. The evidence they'd collected thus far was slim. They couldn't even conclusively prove the man responsible for Julianna's death was the same one who'd murdered Lauren and kidnapped Hayley.

Walker believed they were the same. His gut said they were. But that wasn't proof. Chief Garcia relied on evidence, which made his job harder. "The police are working hard on the case."

"I know they are." Richard glanced past Walker and lifted his hand in a wave.

A moment later, a lanky teen with glasses and a tangle of brown hair joined them. She handed her backpack to Richard and kissed his cheek. "Hey, Dad. We can go."

"Okay, sweetie." He hooked her backpack over his shoulder. "Lily, I'd like you to meet two former students of mine. This is Hayley Barlow and Walker Montgomery." Richard smiled at Hayley. "My daughter, Lily."

"Lovely to meet you." Hayley gave the young girl a sincere smile.

"Likewise." Lily nodded politely. Then she tugged on her dad's sleeve. "Mom's gonna get mad if we're late for piano practice."

"Right. Gotta run." Richard waved bye. Then he and Lily disappeared into the parking lot.

Hayley let out an audible breath. "The guy gives me weird vibes, but he was really great with his daughter." She rubbed her forehead. "We're reading too much into things. There's a reason cops aren't supposed to work cases we're personally involved in. We can't see things clearly."

She had a point. Walker had vacillated between suspecting Richard and wondering if he was imagining things, all in a few minutes. "Did the librarian say where we can find a copy of *Wuthering Heights*?"

"Yeah. It's in the classic section."

Hayley led the way to a corner on the far side of the library. Large tinted windows overlooked the alley running between buildings. Shelves were filled to the brim with neatly organized novels, and a lone table with a couple of chairs rested nearby. The area was impeccably clean but still smelled a touch musty.

Walker sneezed. His cowboy hat shifted on his head and he resettled it.

"Bless you," Hayley said absently as she scanned the section. "Oh, there it is." She pointed to a book on the top-most shelf. "Can you reach it for me, Walker?"

"Sure."

The novel was bound in blue fabric. It scraped against the books alongside as Walker pulled it off the shelf. He extended it toward Hayley when movement from the window caught his attention. His head swiveled.

Aaron Parker. It'd been years since Walker had last seen the high school bully, but he recognized the man instantly from the mug shots. He was bulky and muscular, dark hair wet from the rain, a beard covering the bottom half of his face. His gaze clashed with Walker's through the pane of glass. The hostility in his eyes was shocking.

Then Aaron turned and took off.

Walker dropped the book, his feet automatically moving for the exit. "Stay here, Hails."

He bolted after the criminal.

SIXTEEN

Shock vibrated through Hayley as Walker disappeared around the corner. She glanced out the window but noticed nothing unusual. She took a step to follow him. Her heel caught on *Wuthering Heights*. An envelope with her name on it had fallen out of the book. It rested on the beige carpet like a bad omen.

Indecision warred within her. She didn't want Walker running toward danger without someone to watch his back. At the same time, Hayley couldn't leave the letter on the library floor either. The classic section didn't appear popular with patrons, but that wasn't a guarantee. Someone—like a librarian—could toss the letter in the trash.

Muttering under her breath, she took another look out the window. Still no sign of trouble. Hayley pulled a set of gloves out of her jacket pocket. She took photographs and then retrieved the envelope from the floor.

Inside was another plain sheet of white letter paper. Random symbols, like a circle and wavy lines were scrawled in random intervals. A cross was on the top right. There were no instructions. Hayley flipped the page over, but there was nothing written on the back.

She stared at the sheet dumbfounded, frustration building under her sternum. What on earth was she supposed to do with this? Maybe Walker was right and Casanova had sent them on a wild goose chase.

Hayley's gaze snapped to the window again. No sign of Walker or anyone else in the alley behind the library. Her heart skipped a beat. If this was a trick to get Hayley and Walker to the library, then whatever he'd seen was designed to lure him outside.

A trap.

God, no!

The sound of breaking glass pitched Hayley's heart into overdrive. Screams followed, punctuated by more shattering windows. An unnatural blue vapor plumed across the library like an ominous fog. Smoke bombs. Designed to create confusion and panic.

Hayley shoved the envelope and letter into her pocket. She lifted her shirt over her nose and mouth. The lights hadn't gone out in the library, but it was nearly impossible to see through the thick layer of gas. Her vision blurred. Sirens erupted as the smoke detectors blared.

She moved into the main part of the library. It was pandemonium as patrons desperately tried to find the exits. Explosions came from the far side of the building. Not gunshots. Fireworks.

More screams erupted. Hayley couldn't tell where the assault was coming from. Outside? Or was the assailant inside? The rate at which the lit fireworks were thrown indicated more than one person involved. But that didn't make sense. Casanova worked alone.

Sparks flickered on a shelf. A row of books went up in flames.

Hayley's gut clenched tight. The identity of the person—or people—attacking the library had to take a back seat. It was imperative to get everyone out before the building became an inferno.

As if to punctuate the thought, the fire greedily climbed the entire shelf. Within seconds, it was licking the roof, eating its way through the flammable books. This time, it was gray smoke that flooded the space.

Walker. Had he come back into the library? Or was he lying hurt somewhere outside? She didn't know, and it was terrifying. Hayley sent up a prayer for his safety. Then she concentrated on the task ahead. Every second counted. While she wasn't in law enforcement or the military anymore, Hayley was trained to handle emergency situations. Her focus had to be on saving lives.

A group of teens were huddling in the aisle between shelves of books. Hayley grabbed the kid closest to her. "You need to clear out of the building." She yelled the instructions to be heard over the sound of the smoke alarms and pointed to the red emergency exit sign faintly glowing through the haze. "That way. Hold hands to make sure no one gets lost."

She made sure they headed for the exit before turning her attention to the other aisles. Sweat coated her back. Hayley located a mother and little girl hiding in the kids' section. She directed them to another emergency exit. The fire was spreading quickly. It'd only been two minutes since the initial assault. Thankfully, most of the people fled on their own.

Where was the emergency response? The library was in the center of town. It shouldn't take the police or firefighters so long to get there. Then again, their response might have been delayed if they believed the original source of the attack was a bomb. It would take time to coordinate a plan that minimized the risk to both emergency responders and civilians.

Hayley tossed the absent thought aside and kept moving between the shelves. She found another kid and sent him toward the exit. The flames grew hotter. It roared louder than her heart as it chewed a path along the far wall of the library.

The broken windows let cold air in to feed the flames but also provided a pathway for the smoke to flee. As a result, a thin haze coated everything inside. Hayley's lungs hurt. She wanted to dive into the parking lot and gulp in fresh air, but there was one more group of kids hiding under a table.

She raced to them. A girl and a boy. Junior high schoolers,

judging by their youthful cheeks. The boy's glasses hung askew from his nose. Sweat poured down his forehead and his gaze was wide with terror. He gripped the girl's arm in his hand and was desperately trying to pull her from under the table. When Hayley dropped to her knees, he screamed, "Rachel won't move!"

The girl stared at the flames rapidly approaching her hiding place with a blank stare. She was in shock. Frozen. Hayley's mind superimposed Lauren's face over the teenager's. Time seemed to bend and shift. For a heartbeat, she was back in the car, the feel of a gun barrel pressing against her spine, icy air from the open car door riffling her hair as she tried to shove an unmoving Lauren from the vehicle at a traffic light.

Hayley blinked. The roar of the growing fire, the screaming of the smoke detectors, and the increasing heat brought her back to the moment. She focused on the young boy, pointing to the exit closest to them. "Get to the exit. Rachel and I will be right behind you."

It was the only signal the smart kid needed. He took off like a gazelle being chased by a lion. The glow of daylight flashed as he slipped out of the burning building to safety.

Rachel still hadn't moved. Her expression was blank.

The heat from the flames singed Hayley's skin. She was still wearing her jacket and sweat coated the fabric of her T-shirt. Grabbing the young girl's arms, she shook her. "Rachel. We need to get out of here."

No response. Okay, they'd do it the hard way.

Hayley forcibly dragged the girl out from under the table. Something snapped inside Rachel. She began fighting, but her frantic movements failed to land any significant hit. Hayley understood the young girl's terror and sympathized with it, but now was not the time for comfort. She got into Rachel's face. "Listen to me. We're going to die if we don't move. On your feet."

The order cut through the child's panic. Rachel allowed Hayley to yank her to a standing position. Together, they hurried toward the door. It opened and someone slipped inside. At first glance, Hayley thought it was a firefighter. Then she saw the mask.

Casanova.

She reached for her weapon secure at her hip. Her fingers brushed against the leather holster as she shoved Rachel behind her.

Without a word, Casanova lifted his hand and something whizzed out. Prongs slammed into Hayley's leg and her body jolted as electricity gripped her muscles. Pain exploded in her brain. The hand holding Rachel's arm clamped down uncontrollably, and the two of them tumbled to the carpet as Hayley's knees folded. Her heart thundered against her ribs. The tempo was hard and fast, the world narrowing to that single organ. She couldn't breathe. Couldn't think beyond the white-hot agony.

The current stopped flowing through her body as quickly as it started. Hayley gasped in a breath of smoke-ladened air. Her muscles trembled. In her periphery, Casanova drew closer. It was straight out of her nightmares. His mask was ghost white, a hard plastic shell with a sharp nose, pointy chin, and no mouth. His eyes were cavernous holes.

She trembled. Her body was too weak for complicated movements, but her brain unscrambled enough to recognize the immense trouble she was in. Rachel let out a sob. Hayley's hand was still wrapped around her arm. The girl could escape, but she was frozen with fear and indecision.

Casanova ignored the teen. He bent down next to Hayley. A gloved hand brushed against her cheek. "My sweetheart."

Hayley wanted to recoil from his touch. Instead, she held still, willing the fingers on her other hand to form a fist. A part of her was tempted to let Casanova take her. He was holding Kelly somewhere. Maybe he'd take Hayley there too and she could help the other woman. Except... that would leave Rachel inside the burning library.

It was an impossible choice, but there was only one answer. Rachel was here. Now. Her life had to take precedence.

Please, God, give me strength.

Hayley couldn't maneuver her fingers to operate her handgun, still holstered at the small of her back. Not after being shocked with the stun gun. There was only one option available to get out of this. One chance. It had to work.

Casanova rose, as if to slide his hands under Hayley's body to lift her. She tightened her fist and willed her muscles to give everything they had.

Then she punched him in the groin.

He crumpled to the ground. A swear word wheezed from his lips, and somewhere in the back of Hayley's mind, she registered a familiar voice. But there was no time to consider it. She pulled the stun gun's prongs from her leg. Then she staggered to her feet and tugged Rachel into a standing position. "Run! Run!"

The girl didn't seem to register the words. Hayley's knees threatened to give way again, but she lurched toward the exit on unsteady feet, pulling and tugging Rachel behind her.

The emergency exit door opened again. Walker appeared just as Hayley shoved Rachel outside. The teen finally took off down the alley toward the street.

Hayley nearly collapsed in Walker's arms. Her relief at his arrival was short lived. She gulped in the scent of fresh air pouring through the open doorway. Her brain wasn't operating correctly, and her muscles quaked. Still, she eked out one word. "Casanova."

She glanced over her shoulder, expecting to see the killer still on the library floor.

He was gone.

SEVENTEEN

He'd messed up.

Walker mentally berated himself for leaving Hayley in the library to chase after Aaron. The slippery criminal disappeared before he could catch up to him in the alley and then the streets flooded with law enforcement just as the attack on the library happened. It'd been pandemonium. Casanova had nearly kidnapped Hayley during the confusion.

It'd been hours since Walker had pulled Hayley from the library, but his heart rate hadn't returned to normal.

He'd nearly lost her.

As if she read his thoughts, Hayley placed her hand over his under the kitchen table. He immediately interlaced their fingers. Her hair was damp from a recent shower and the scent of her shampoo—that intoxicating tropical fragrance with traces of coconut and mango—tickled Walker's senses. The emergency room doctor had prescribed rest, but Hayley insisted on joining the team meeting. She was desperate to find Kelly. They all were.

Gathered around the table were Walker's friends. Pizza boxes were scattered throughout the kitchen, most of them empty, and the scents of basil and tomato sauce hung heavy in the air. The serious-ness of the day had cast a shadow over their dinner, but one thing soldiers knew was that battle required fuel. They couldn't work on empty stomachs.

Boone and Connor were sleeping under the table. Both of them had gorged on doggie treats.

"An individual called the police station and reported there were several bombs planted around town." Tucker scraped a hand through his hair and the auburn strands stood on end. Dark circles marred the skin under his eyes, and he smelled like a chimney from the library fire. Unlike Walker and Hayley, he hadn't had a chance to shower. "One at the library, one at the Blessed Hearts Youth Center, another at Knoxville High School, and a final at Nelson's Diner. We immedi-ately scrambled to evacuate those places, but before we could, the attack on the library happened."

Hayley's mouth dropped open. "No wonder it took first respon-ders so long."

Tucker nodded. "Without knowing if there was more than one bomb, patrol began clearing the adjacent buildings. We called the sheriff's department for backup, but it took time for them to arrive." He blew out a breath. "Thankfully, the bomb threats for all the other locations were fake."

"Still terrifying though." Logan glowered. His wife ran Blessed Hearts Youth Center, so the bomb threat had hit close to home. Like Tucker, the paramedic was still dressed in his uniform. He also smelled like a chimney. An empty plate with a smear of pizza sauce and a dirty napkin sat in front of him.

"Smart." Jason leaned back in his chair. Connor popped one eye open to make sure his master didn't need him, and when Jason stayed seated, he went back to sleep. "Casanova calls in the bomb threat to keep the police busy and then attacks the library with smoke bombs and firecrackers to create panic while he kidnaps Hayley. That's a well-coordinated plan. Whoever this guy is, he's organized."

"We already knew that," Walker pointed out. "He's murdered at least two people—Lauren and Julianna—and is suspected of killing eight other women. Not to mention kidnapping Kelly. Casanova hasn't gotten away with his crimes for this long by being sloppy." He turned back to Tucker. "Did Chief Garcia question Bobby Ray?"

"He did. Bobby Ray claims he had nothing to do with the attack on the library or the recent murders. He hasn't spoken or heard from his half-brother Aaron in years, and didn't know he was in town. According to Bobby Ray, his father did cheat on his mom. He doesn't know how many half-siblings may be running around."

Logan snorted. "So basically hear no evil, see no evil."

"Pretty much. Since he's on parole, law enforcement can search his residence at any time. The chief tore apart Bobby Ray's apartment but didn't find any evidence linking him to the crimes or Aaron."

Hayley's eyebrows shot up. "Wait a minute. Bobby Ray doesn't live with his mother?"

"Nope."

"So he could be hiding stuff on his mom's property." She stiffened. "Kelly could be there right now."

"Yes, but without probable cause, we can't search Regina Daniels's residence." Tucker drained the last of his coffee and set the mug on the table. "Her criminal son visiting isn't enough. We need some evidence proving Kelly is being held on the property." Tucker frowned. "Honestly, Bobby Ray could be telling the truth. Aaron was the one outside the library. He ran away but might've doubled back after losing Walker."

"They could be working together." Walker's mind whirled with the possibility.

"It's something to consider." Hayley released Walker's hand and rose to collect the carafe from the coffee machine. She refilled Tucker's mug and topped off a few others. "It's possible the attack on the library was carried out by just one person, but it would've been easier with two. Bobby Ray and Aaron may have teamed up."

Tucker tilted his head. "That would be rare for this kind of crime. Serial killers typically work alone. Plus, divulging his identity—even to his half-brother—would put Casanova at risk. The more people who know, the greater the chance someone will turn on him."

"True, but Bobby Ray and Aaron have teamed up before. They ran in the same crowd in high school and committed crimes together. It's not outside the realm of possibility they're in this together."

"Hayley makes a good point." Jason crossed his arms. "I find it difficult to believe Aaron popped back up in Knoxville after years of living in Houston right as all this trouble starts. He's got to be involved."

"Maybe, but it's like you said, these crimes are well-planned." Tucker shook his head. "I don't think Bobby Ray or Aaron have the brains to pull something like this off. Their rap sheets are long, but they aren't criminal masterminds. Casanova is smart, patient, and adept at hiding his identity. In my opinion, we're looking for someone else."

Walker drummed his fingers on the table. "Thomas might have more children. It's also possible Casanova isn't a member of the Daniels family but wants us to think they are. Chris Wallaby was friends with Bobby Ray and Aaron for a time. He could be working with Aaron."

Hayley frowned. "There's no evidence of that. While Chris made mistakes in his teens, he's made amends for them. I don't like the idea of using those screwups against him now."

Nathan cleared his throat. "I did some additional digging on Chris and found something of interest. Before working as a security guard for the high school, he drove trucks for a regional grocery store." He pointed to the corkboard still propped up next to the window. The faces of Casanova's suspected victims stared back. "Chris's route took him right through the counties where the other women were killed. He couldn't stalk them in that moment—truck drivers have strict schedules—but it would've given him an opportunity to identify a victim and then stalk her during his personal time. If nothing else, it gives him a familiarity with the areas."

Jason whistled, his facial scar pulling with the movement. "Well, we can't knock Chris off the suspect list then. He knows Hayley. Admitted to knowing Julianna too. Did you find any evidence linking him to any of the other victims?"

"No, but I'm still in the early stages. I'll need more time."

Walker nodded and then turned to Kyle. Chris wasn't the only person who knew Hayley and Julianna. "What about Richard Westbrook?"

"Not a blemish on his record." Kyle cracked his knuckles and then stretched them. "Richard's been married for the last fifteen years. One daughter, Lily, twelve. Parents are deceased. Owns his own home. Worked as a math teacher in San Antonio before accepting a job at Knoxville High School. Richard became the principal last year. I spoke to a couple of his former colleagues in San Antonio. They described him as off,"—he put air quotes around off— "but relatively boring."

Hayley leaned on the table. "What did they mean by off?"

"It's not clear. Several women described him as strange but couldn't pinpoint why. I got the impression he's socially awkward. Richard says things in the wrong tone or at the wrong time and it can be off-putting to folks."

Walker could see that. He'd had a similar experience with the man. "Any hints of violence in his past?"

"Nope. His former colleagues have never seen him lose his temper." Kyle opened a pizza box and snagged a slice. "I can dig for a connection between Aaron and Richard outside of a student/teacher one. But if you're asking me, I don't think Richard should be at the top of our suspect list. Bobby Ray, however, is a different story. He's related to Aaron and has access to his family's property."

"Agreed, but right now, we can't eliminate anyone. All we have are theories." Frustration nipped at him. Walker planted his hands on his hips. "Let's call it a night and regroup in the morning. We'll think better with some sleep."

"I feel wide awake." Jason stood. Connor immediately rose from his slumber and belly crawled out from under the table to sit by his owner's side. Jason patted the dog's head. "In fact, I could stay up all night. Hey, Kyle, what do you think about a stakeout?" He grinned. "Let's see if we can catch Bobby Ray doing something illegal."

"Only if you buy me breakfast in the morning." Kyle shoved the last bite of pizza in his mouth.

Nathan shook his head. "I swear, you would do anything for a meal."

"Not anything." Kyle grinned at his cousin. "Just most things."

Everyone laughed. Walker shot Jason a grateful look, and the former Marine nodded in acknowledgement. If Bobby Ray was Casanova and had Kelly, then a stakeout could lead Jason and Kyle to her. Right now, it was their best hope for finding the woman alive.

Although Walker feared they were already too late.

Jason and Kyle left, followed by Tucker and Logan. Nathan had first watch on the ranch. He disappeared into the darkness after saying goodnight to Hayley and Walker. They headed for the main house. The night sky loomed over them, sprinkled with a thick blanket of stars.

Hayley hooked a hand through the crook of Walker's arm. "Are you okay?"

He pulled her closer. "I'm supposed to be asking you that question. You're the one that came face-to-face with Casanova." Walker's chest clenched. He didn't want to think about how close he'd come to losing her forever. "What you did was incredibly brave. You saved lives today. Not just Rachel's. All the people you directed out of the building."

She glanced at him and then the moon. "It felt good. Using my skills to help others. I'd forgotten how much purpose it brings me." Hayley rubbed the fingers of her right hand together. The scars from her old wound were barely visible in the dim light. "I miss being in law enforcement, but after this... I'm not sure I want to face down people like Casanova daily anymore. I've had so much sadness in my life. It's exhausting."

Walker couldn't blame her. Hayley hadn't just been through a traumatic experience with Casanova. Her entire childhood had been chaotic. He wrapped an arm around her shoulders and tugged her closer. "You'll find your way. There's no need to decide the future now."

She laughed. "That's the wisest thing you've said all night."

Her tone was teasing. Walker reached between their bodies with his other hand and tickled Hayley's side. She squealed and then jumped away before racing up the porch steps. Her giggles were music to his ears.

Walker followed her into the warm kitchen. His mom was standing at the stove, heating a bottle, baby Sophia in her arms. The little girl had been crying. Her face was red.

"Poor thing looks mad," Walker noted, shucking his jacket.

"She's hungry." Aileen pushed the baby in his direction. "Can you hold her for one minute? I need to change her bedding. Her diaper didn't contain everything, and the crib is a mess."

Walker quickly washed his hands and then took the baby from his mom. Aileen rushed from the room, her nightgown flapping around her ankles.

Sophia whimpered and Walker rocked her side to side. The little tike was wearing purple pjs, her dark hair curling around her sweet face. She blinked her blue eyes. Her expression was wary. Walker smiled. "I think she's concerned about herself. I must look scary."

Hayley chuckled, drawing closer. "Naw. She's studying your face." Her hand cupped the back of the baby's head. "She's adorable. It's hard to remember the world is a scary place when Sophia's around."

Their gazes met. Walker's heart picked up speed. This close, the details of Hayley's eyes were distinguishable. The various shades tangled together in a sea of warm brown. Whips of dark hair played with the delicate curves of her face. The woman was stunning. Brave. Tough yet caring.

Walker hadn't considered marriage or children since returning home, convinced that Lauren's death had scarred him so badly, he couldn't imagine having little ones of his own. Now, staring into Hayley's eyes, the undeniable truth hit him with the force of a fist to the solar plexus.

He didn't want anyone else but her.

Hayley's gaze sought his with silent questions. Walker couldn't find the words to tell her what he was thinking. The timing was all wrong. Casanova was still out there. Kelly was missing. Hayley had already told him she was leaving Knoxville for good after this case was over. But he couldn't focus on any of that. All he could imagine was standing in the kitchen with Hayley, holding their child in his arms. The longing was intense.

He lifted a hand and cupped her cheek. His thumb grazed her lip. Hayley inhaled sharply, her eyes darkening with want and need. She drew closer, rising on her tiptoes. It was all the invitation Walker needed. He leaned forward and pressed his lips to hers.

The world shifted under his feet. Walker's heart took off like Midnight racing from the paddock. Time stretched out and every cell in his body was aware of Hayley. The softness of her lips, the tropical scent of her shampoo, the feel of her hand on his arm and the infant nestled between them.

This... this is what his heart had been asking for.

It was an impossible situation. Asking Hayley to stay was selfish. Walker couldn't do it. She'd been through so much and deserved a fresh start. A new life.

One without him.

EIGHTEEN

The next morning, Hayley rocked Sophia on the front porch swing. The baby was bundled for the weather in several layers and a fleece-lined blanket. A hat covered her little head. Long lashes rested on plump cheeks. Boone raced in the yard, chasing squirrels with abandon.

Inside the kitchen, visible through the window, Shane and Aileen were chatting over breakfast. The older couple shared a laugh. Then Aileen patted her husband's leg cast before leaning over to kiss him sweetly.

Hayley averted her gaze from the intimate moment. Only to once again have her attention drawn back to Walker in the paddock. She'd been trying to avoid watching him work with Midnight for the last half hour. And failing miserably. His tall, broad-shouldered form was like a beacon, and all Hayley could think about was the kiss they'd shared last night.

It'd been magical. There was no other word for it.

Walker's voice carried on the wind. His tone was low and soothing. The large Percheron hadn't allowed Walker to touch him, but he wasn't running away either. Ollie, a gentle and patient quarter horse, was also in the corral. She ate up Walker's affection while Midnight stood nearby. Hayley had the sense he was thinking about stepping closer to Walker but hadn't gotten up the courage. It was a feeling she could relate to.

Hayley didn't know what to do about her relationship with Walker. Things had been emotional since Casanova's return and the attack at the library had heightened matters further. Had the kiss just been a tender moment between exes? Or was it something more?

The wisest course of action was to catalog the moment as a misstep and maintain a steady course of action. Capture Casanova, sell her mom's house, leave Knoxville. One romantic kiss didn't erase all the reasons a relationship between them was impossible.

So why did the idea of driving away from Walker make Hayley want to cry?

She shoved the thoughts aside and focused on the paper in her hand. It was a copy of Casanova's drawing left in *Wuthering Heights*. The original had been taken into evidence by Tucker last night, along with the other notes. No fingerprints were found on them. Of course. Casanova wasn't foolish enough to handle the papers or envelopes without gloves.

She'd spent most of the night studying the weird shapes and wavy lines but couldn't make sense of them. It likely meant nothing. Casanova had intended to kidnap Hayley from the library. He hadn't intended for her to ever find Kelly.

An SUV rounded a bend in the driveway, Nathan at the wheel. Cassie was in the passenger seat next to him. She gave a wave to Hayley as her husband parked. All four doors on the SUV opened. Tucker and Leah exited the back seat.

Today, Tucker was in plain clothes. Must be a day off. Well deserved too. He'd been working nonstop since Hayley brought the case to the Knoxville Police Department.

Hayley rose to greet them.

"Oh, my goodness, let me have that little nugget." Leah, curly hair bouncing, raced toward Hayley, her arms extended and her hands waving in a gimme gesture. Her hazel eyes shimmered with happiness behind her glasses when Hayley handed over Sophia. Leah arranged the blanket around the infant. She breathed in. "She smells so sweet. I can't get enough of this baby."

Tucker wrapped an arm around his wife's waist. A smile played on his lips. "You might want to say hi to Hayley before yanking Sophia from her arms."

Leah blushed. "Oh, yeah. Sorry. Hi, Hayley."

Hayley laughed. Leah had been over almost every day since Sophia's arrival. She definitely had baby fever, but it was touching to watch. She and Tucker were a wonderful couple, and they were going to make fantastic parents one day. "Don't worry about it, Leah. Sophia's so cute. I don't blame you for focusing on her." She turned to Tucker. "Any news?"

His smile faltered. "No. Jason and Kyle watched Bobby Ray all night. He never moved from his apartment. There's still no sign of Kelly. Chief Garcia hasn't stopped searching. He's opened a tip line and is running down every lead."

Hayley nodded. Everyone hoped to find Kelly alive, but with every hour that passed, it became less and less likely. "There's been no word from Casanova either."

"He's licking his wounds," Nathan offered.

"Maybe." She feared he was taking his anger out on Kelly. Hayley couldn't stay in that headspace though. It wasn't productive. "Walker and I are going to review the cases again from the start. Maybe we'll find something new that'll crack this investigation wide open."

"Great idea." Nathan smacked Tucker's chest. "We can help."

"It's getting colder." Leah eyed the dark clouds drifting in to block the sun. "I'm going to take this little bundle of love inside."

"I'll catch up with you later." Tucker brushed a kiss along her hairline. "Say hi to Walker's parents for me."

The group split, going in different directions. Leah disappeared inside the house with the baby while Nathan and Tucker headed for the paddock to speak to Walker. Hayley was still holding Casanova's note. She showed it to Cassie.

The blonde-haired beauty studied it for a long moment. Then she shook her head. "I don't know, Hayley. It sorta looks like a topical map, but that could be just because of this circle with wavy lines. None of the other symbols are right." Cassie frowned. She turned the page one way and then the other. "It's really strange."

"Considering Casanova intended to kidnap me last night, this note may mean nothing. Thanks for looking anyway." Hayley gestured toward Walker, who was still in the paddock with Midnight. Tucker and Nathan hung on the fence, watching as the large horse considered his options. "Midnight's making progress."

"He is." Cassie smiled and adjusted her cowboy hat. Then she glanced at Hayley and her grin faltered. She shifted in her boots. "I'm glad we have a quiet moment to talk. I've been wanting to tell you something. Maybe this isn't the right time, but..." She shrugged. "When is, right?"

Hayley waited, letting the other woman sort out her thoughts.

"Your mom used to work on my ranch from time to time," Cassie continued. "Odd jobs here and there. Nothing permanent. But we kept in contact. I'm not sure if you're aware, but she started attending Narcotics Anonymous. Church too. Janet wanted to get her life right."

Shock vibrated through Hayley. "She didn't tell me."

"I encouraged her to. Janet talked a lot about you, about the mistakes she made in raising you. She regretted her choices and didn't want to involve you until she was certain sobriety would stick." Her gaze drifted some place over Hayley's shoulder. "I know the official cause of death was overdose. I debated saying anything... I didn't want to upset you. But ultimately, I thought you should know that while Janet made a horrible choice in that moment, she was working on being a better person. A better mom."

Hayley's chin trembled as emotion swelled. Words couldn't eke past the lump in her throat. All she'd ever wanted was a meaningful relationship with her mother. It was heartbreaking to realize it'd been so close and yet didn't happen. She swallowed. "I should've called her more. Checked in. I was..."

Protecting herself. From the hurt and destruction her mom's addiction wreaked on everything around her.

Cassie gently placed a hand on her arm. "She understood. Janet was proud of you."

Hayley swiped at the tears on her cheeks. Shucks, she was crying again. The waterworks hadn't stopped since she crossed the town line into Knoxville. "Thank you for telling me. It makes a difference to know she was trying."

"I'm glad." Sympathy shone in Cassie's eyes. "I didn't have a good relationship with my mom either. She abandoned me when I was a kid, and for a long time, I struggled with not feeling good enough. Relationships with parents can be complicated. Don't beat yourself up for making choices you needed to."

Hayley blew out a breath. "You've struggled with not feeling good enough?" It was hard to imagine. Cassie was a bright and sensitive person who carried herself with such confidence. "I never would've guessed."

Her gaze shifted to the paddock. The men were still waiting patiently for Midnight to make his move. Hayley debated divulging her innermost fears to Cassie, but after the moment they'd just shared, it felt appropriate. "I've battled that feeling my whole life. Like my mom's addiction had something to do with me. Which I know seems strange, but..." She didn't know how to express what she was feeling.

"If you were enough, then she'd get clean."

"Yes." The knots binding Hayley's chest loosened, and for the first time in a long time, it felt like she could breathe better. "But it's more complicated than that. My childhood was messed up and then this stuff with Casanova... it feels like I'm not meant to be happy. Like the normal stuff—marriage and kids—aren't meant for someone like me."

Cassie was silent for a long moment. Then she lifted her chin toward the paddock. "You and Midnight are a lot alike. He's got every reason in the world not to trust Walker, based on how others have treated him. But he wants to. You can see it in the way his body is poised." She turned back to Hayley. "I've been there. Wanting to trust, but terrified at the same time. What you and Midnight don't know—and what I've learned—is that loving the right person changes everything."

Hayley bit her lip. "No matter what Walker does, no matter how deep his love, it can't remove Midnight's scars."

"No, but we all carry scars. Some are visible, others not." Cassie's tone was kind. "Midnight's are obvious, but once he learns to trust, once he realizes he's safe, those scars will be a visible testament to the challenges he overcame. Nothing more."

She touched the tattoo etched on the inner part of her wrist. There was a lot of truth in Cassie's words. Hayley sighed. "You make it sound so easy."

Cassie chuckled. "Uh, no. It's difficult. But it gets easier the more you listen to God. Trust where He's leading you." She linked an arm through Hayley's and together they started walking toward the paddock. "Of course, I don't promise there won't be storm clouds now and again." She hip bumped Hayley. "But that's why you have friends who can remind you to pray."

Hayley hip bumped her back with a laugh. Then her gaze caught on Walker and she slid to a stop, yanking Cassie to a halt with her. "Look," she whispered, pointing toward Midnight.

The horse had lifted his foot. He set it down again but shuffled as if unsure.

Collectively, it felt like everyone was holding their breath. Hayley was transfixed by the horse. By Walker. He was petting Ollie, completely ignoring Midnight, but was aware of the horse's indecision. He shifted his body closer. Continued to praise Ollie in that soothing voice of his.

Midnight lifted his foot again. Cassie held Hayley's hands in both of hers. They both leaned forward as if willing the horse to move.

He stepped toward Walker.

Cassie pinched her mouth shut and swallowed back a yelp. Hayley's own excitement jittered across her body. Then, without looking at Midnight, Walker reached out a hand. His fingers brushed against the horse's muzzle.

Midnight took another step toward him.

Hayley's heart soared. Once again, tears sprang to her eyes and she let them fall, not caring anymore about keeping her emotions in check. Cassie was crying too. They watched for a few minutes while Walker stroked and talked to Midnight. Then he released both horses into the pasture. He sported a large grin as he greeted Tucker and Nathan. Cassie hugged him before her husband edged her out of the way.

"Well done!" Nathan clapped Walker on the back.

The two men shared a brotherly hug and then Walker shoved his friend. "Told you I was good with horses."

They wrestled for a moment and then Walker broke away. Hayley sucked in a breath as their gazes met. He came toward her on long strides, his eyes shining with warmth. For her. No matter what their future held, she would remember this moment for the rest of her life. Hayley ran across the distance between them, throwing herself into his arms.

Walker caught her easily. Lifted her feet off the ground and spun her in a circle. "Did you see that?"

"Every second." She looped her arms around his neck. He smelled of horse and hard work. "You did good, cowboy."

He brushed his lips against hers. The kiss was featherlight but sweet and full of unspoken words. Then he set Hayley on her feet, his hands encircling her waist. His gaze drifted to the ground. "What's this?"

Walker released her to pick up the paper that'd fallen out of her pocket.

All at once, reality came crashing down on Hayley. Kelly was still missing. She unfolded the sheet. "It's the note Casanova left in *Wuthering Heights*. I keep thinking it means something. Cassie thought it looked like a topical map because of this circle with the wavy lines, but she said all the other symbols are wrong."

Walker's head tilted. "A topical map... Hold on..." He grabbed Hayley's hand and started pulling her to the house. "I have an idea." He yelled behind him. "Nathan, your wife may be a genius."

Hayley raced to keep up with Walker. The screen door slammed shut multiple times as everyone piled into the house. Leah was in the kitchen with Walker's parents, still holding Sophia. They came into the living room to see what all the fuss was about.

Walker went straight to the office built in an alcove off his parents' dining room. He fired up the computer and accessed a map of Knoxville. "Cassie's right. The symbols aren't technically right for a topical map, but it might've been drawn by an amateur." He clicked the mouse. Then handed Hayley the letter. "Hold this in front of the computer screen like this while I adjust the map."

Her heart picked up speed as the squiggle lines and strange shapes shifted into focus. She inhaled. "They're landmarks." Crudely drawn, but the lake was obvious, as was the highway. Hayley pointed to the shape she'd mistaken for a cross or a T.

It was a misshapen X.

"X marks the spot," she whispered. "Walker, where is this?"

His gaze shot to her face. The excitement drained from his eyes. "It's the cemetery."

Disappointment and pain flooded through her. Casanova was

playing a cruel joke. She glanced down at the note in her hand and a whisper of something drifted through her. Hayley couldn't shake the feeling there was more to it than that.

"It doesn't make sense. Why did Casanova leave a note for me in the envelope if he intended to kidnap me from the library? There's no way I could follow the map..." Hayley inhaled sharply. "It's not meant for me." She met Walker's questioning gaze. "This note was meant for *you*."

His eyes widened. "He wanted me to find Kelly after you'd been taken."

Emotional and mental torture. Casanova wasn't just trying to hurt Hayley, he wanted Walker to hurt too. "The cemetery has lots of places to hide a person. It's full of mausoleums and other buildings." Her heart picked up speed. "Kelly could still be alive. He could be holding her there because his plan went awry and he's figuring out his next move."

Sympathy creased his brow. "Hails..."

"No." The word came out sharp. Hayley was suddenly aware of the group of people behind her, but she didn't care if she sounded stupid or foolish. "We don't give up hope. Until we know Kelly is dead for sure, we do everything possible to save her."

Walker's mouth firmed, and then he nodded sharply. "You're right." He glanced over his shoulder. "Tucker, we'll need something with Kelly's scent on it. Nathan, call Jason. Have him and Connor meet us at the cemetery ASAP. We've got a new lead to chase."

NINETEEN

Storm clouds hung heavy over Knoxville Cemetery, casting the headstones and mausoleums in shrouds of dark gray. Some graves went back hundreds of years. Family genealogists would pop in occasionally, looking for long-lost relatives buried in the family tombs that dotted the landscape among the ancient oak and pecan trees. The cemetery was so old, cars couldn't drive along the main pathway. It was too narrow. Everyone had to walk.

Walker had been here several times—mostly to lay flowers on his grandparents' graves as well as Lauren's—and never had an issue. This time, however, with the approaching thunderstorm scattering leaves, and Casanova's potential victim hidden among the gravestones, the cemetery gave him the willies.

He glanced at Hayley. She was bundled in a thick coat, shoulders hunched against the wind. A pink scarf encased her neck and brought out the rosy color of her cheeks. Her lips were chapped again. Determination set her jaw and her gaze never stopped assessing their immediate area.

Walker sensed her need to move. To search. The odds of finding Kelly alive weren't in their favor. It would be Casanova's style to leave the murdered woman in a cemetery. The guy was a psycho. His plan to kidnap Hayley from the library had gone down the drain, but Walker wasn't foolish enough to believe he was done. In fact, he imagined Casanova would take pleasure in Hayley finding Kelly.

But how would she handle it? Hayley was one of the toughest people Walker had ever met, but everyone had a breaking point.

"Is it me or is this place creepy?" Jason strolled across the parking lot to the cemetery entrance on long strides. Connor kept pace at his side. The German shepherd had once been a bomb detection dog in the military. An IED explosion ended that career, but in the last few years, Jason trained Connor for Search and Rescue operations.

Tucker frowned. "Definitely creepy. Of course, we're following instructions from a serial killer, so that could taint matters." He held a sealed evidence bag in one hand. "I grabbed a shirt from the dirty clothes hamper at Kelly's house. I also have socks, if you need."

"The shirt should be enough." Jason snapped a harness on Connor.

The dog was always obedient, but the moment the harness was in place, his ears pitched forward and his attention became laser focused on his owner. Walker hadn't worked much with military or SAR dogs, but he knew the basics. The vest was a signal to Connor that it was time to work.

Jason took the evidence bag from Tucker, opened it, and then let Connor sniff the clothing. He gave the order to find. The German shepherd went to the entrance of the cemetery. He lifted his nose and moved in several directions. The dog appeared lost.

Walker frowned. "Will he have an issue finding Kelly with the thunderstorm approaching?"

"The wind is troublesome, but Connor's nose is one of the best I've ever seen. He's trained to use a scent cone, but can also track via the ground through the skin cells we shed all the time. If Kelly is here, he'll find her. Give him a minute."

Seconds later, Connor tore down the main pathway. Jason and

Walker bolted after him, Hayley and Tucker bringing up the rear. Rain peppered Walker's cowboy hat. His boots crunched leaves across the pathway. At some point, Connor deviated onto the grass, maneuvering between gravestones. His bright orange vest was a beacon against the gray stone.

Walker kept one hand on his holstered weapon. The memory of being shot outside the police department replayed in his mind. The cemetery would be a good place for a sniper to hide. His gaze roamed the area constantly, while keeping a visual on Connor's vest.

The dog led the group to an older section of the cemetery. Overgrown grass grew around crumbling headstones in need of repair. A few hopeful wildflowers sprang up here and there despite the frigid temperatures. The rain picked up in intensity.

Tucker unfurled his umbrella. The police officer was in plain clothes but hadn't lost an ounce of his protective nature. He kept close to Hayley, guarding her so that Walker could keep pace with Jason and Connor.

Wind rustled the tree branches and sent the rain slanting sideways. Walker blinked the water off his eyelashes. He picked up the pace as Connor rounded the side of a large mausoleum built in the 20s. Several quick barks followed.

"He's found her." Jason broke into a run.

Walker followed, his boots sliding on the wet grass. Pain shot through his knee, the metal joint protesting the jerky movement. He ignored it. His heart picked up speed as the door to the mausoleum came into view. Connor scratched at the wood and barked again. Jason reached the dog first. He praised Connor as Walker reached for the door handle. The metal was cold against his heated palm. He twisted.

The door gave way immediately, hinges swinging open wide, and Walker stumbled inside. The scent of must and decay assaulted his senses. Aboveground tombs were strategically placed inside the mausoleum. Light filtered in through a stained-glass window on the opposite end from the door. Dust and dirt covered most of the floor, but obvious sweep marks—done by Casanova to erase his footprints—created a path.

A roar sounded in Walker's ears as his heart rate increased. He stepped farther into the darkness. Hayley came up behind him, and he held her back with one hand, desperate to shield her from what was inside. But she wouldn't yield. Instead, she grabbed his arm with her hand and kept pace with him, flicking on her cell phone for brighter illumination.

Blood. On the floor.

Walker stepped to the side, careful to do his best to preserve the evidence, even as he moved deeper into the giant mausoleum. It housed half a dozen family members. The cement was icy, and the sound of Walker's boots bounced around the room as he headed for the pool of blood.

His mind made mental notes in quick snaps as a foot came into view, encased in a house slipper, a dot of blue against pale skin. Walker's breathing shallowed as he rounded the side of an above-ground coffin and Kelly came into view.

She was ghost white, her dark hair casting a halo around her pale face. Jeans covered her long legs, and her sweatshirt was stained with blood. Rose petals were scattered around her. A melted candle, the wick black, sat nearby. Kelly held a bloody hand over her abdomen. She'd been shot. Her eyes were closed.

Hayley inhaled sharply. Her hand flew to her mouth.

Walker dropped to one knee, his fingers automatically pressing against the column of Kelly's throat, seeking a pulse. Her skin was cold to the touch. Lips tinged with blue. The blood on the floor was dark, but on her sweatshirt, it appeared fresher.

A beat thumped against his fingertips.

Hope sprang in Walker's chest and he held still. Another beat. Her pulse was thready and weak, but it was there. "She's alive." He ripped off his jacket and then his long-sleeved shirt. The damp cold sank into his bones, cutting through the thin layer of his undershirt. Walker barely felt it. He balled up the fabric of his long-sleeved shirt and pressed it against Kelly's wound.

Hayley held her phone to her ear. In clipped tones, she told dispatch they needed police and EMS. A moment later, she said, "They're on the way, but it'll take some time to carry Kelly out of here."

Walker gestured for her to hold the shirt against Kelly's wound. "I have a first aid kit in my truck. Tucker and Jason probably have one too." He glanced at the door of the mausoleum, suddenly realizing that neither of his friends had followed them inside, even though Tucker was a police officer. He'd want to secure the scene and preserve as much evidence as possible.

Gunfire erupted.

TWENTY

Hayley's heart leapt to her throat.

Her gaze shot to the door of the mausoleum before returning to Walker. He was already maneuvering around the far side of the aboveground casket, his handgun pulled and at the ready.

"Move to the other side of Kelly, Hayley, and hide behind the casket with her. Keep pressure on that wound. I'm going to assess the situation."

Hayley did as he asked without question. Walker disappeared from view. His footsteps grew softer as he approached the door. Walker wouldn't leave her defenseless, but he also couldn't abandon Tucker and Jason to face a sniper alone. Nor should he. Hayley sent up a prayer for everyone's safety.

Casanova had led them here. Straight into a trap.

She wanted to pull her own weapon but needed both hands to apply hard pressure to the gunshot wound. The icy cement dug into her knees, causing them to ache. The gunshots continued outside. From the sound of it, the sniper was using a rifle. Probably with a scope. He had range and accuracy. Tucker and Jason carried, just like she and Walker did, but a handgun was no match for a long-range rifle.

Her breath hitched as a tinge of panic grew. Hayley was a person of action. Staying still, not knowing what was going on and not being able to help, was triggering. The darkness of the mausoleum and the musty smell of decay reminded her of the shed she'd been held captive in. Drugged. Cold. In pain. Alone.

Don't. She gave herself a mental shake. Losing it right now wasn't an option.

A hand grabbed her arm.

Hayley stifled a scream, her attention shooting down to the woman on the ground. Kelly stared back. Her eyes were wide with terror. She held onto Hayley with a fierce grip that was incredibly strong considering how much blood she'd lost and the trauma she'd been through. Kelly's mouth opened, but nothing came out.

"You're okay." Hayley whispered the words. They were punctuated by more gunshots from outside. "We're going to get you out of here. I need you to hang on, okay? Just keep breathing."

"Cas... casa..."

"Casanova did this. I know." Hayley kept pushing on the woman's wound. "Have you ever seen his face?"

Kelly shook her head no.

"Do you know who he is?"

Another no.

Disappointment stabbed Hayley, but she smothered it back down. The main objective had to be getting everyone out of this situation alive. Casanova had never shown his real identity to her either. His mask was part of his persona.

Kelly trembled and shivered. Walker's jacket covered the woman's petite form, but it wasn't enough protection from the cold.

Hayley removed her hands from the wound. She unzipped her jacket and quickly tugged it off, using the item to cover more of Kelly's shaking form. Then she reapplied pressure. "I need you to stay with me. I know it hurts, but you've gotten this far. Just a little longer, okay?"

Kelly didn't answer. Hayley glanced at the other woman's face.

Her eyes were closed.

Panic set in. Hayley desperately checked for a pulse along the cool column of Kelly's throat. A heartbeat thumped against her fingers. Thin and weak, but it was there. Relief turned Hayley's insides to water. She let go of the breath she was holding and went back to pushing against the wound. Despite the cold temperatures, sweat beaded along her forehead.

The scrape of a boot against concrete echoed through the mausoleum.

Hayley froze. There hadn't been any gunshots outside for a few minutes. Had the sniper injured all three men? Was he coming for her and Kelly now?

Keeping one hand on Kelly, Hayley used the other to unsnap the holster on her weapon. The click sounded incredibly loud to her own ears. Her fingers were coated with blood. She swiped them against her jeans and then pulled her gun. She pointed it. Slowed her breathing to keep the adrenaline from narrowing her vision.

No one was going to hurt Kelly. Not while she had breath in her body.

Another boot scrape. Closer this time.

Hayley held her breath. Her finger slid against the trigger.

"Hails, it's me."

Walker came into view. Grass stained his pants and his hat was missing. He carried his handgun at his side.

Hayley's muscles went limp. She lowered her own gun. "You should've announced yourself at the entrance. I nearly shot you." Then she caught the gleam in his eye, the triumphant smile on his face. "What is it?"

"We got him."

Hours later, Hayley wrapped her hands around a takeaway cup of coffee. Her body didn't need any more caffeine, but the warmth of the liquid eased the block of iciness lodged behind her sternum. The hum of the Knoxville Police Department filtered through the closed door of the break room. Rain beat against the window. Normally a soothing sound, the thunderstorm grated on Hayley's last reserve of nerves. A headache brewed behind her eyes.

Walker appeared in the doorway. They'd separated an hour ago to give their statements. Only sixty minutes apart, but the sight of him sent Hayley's heart rate into overdrive. She rose from her chair. Within seconds, Walker enveloped her in his strong arms. She leaned against his broad chest. Breathed. Relished his solid form under her cheek and the tender way he cupped the back of her head. She was safe. He was safe.

The harrowing moments in the mausoleum after the gunfire broke replayed repeatedly in her head. Jason, Connor, and Tucker were unharmed. Working as a team with Walker, they took the sniper down. Aaron Parker was cooling his heels in an interview room. The first thing he did was ask for a lawyer.

Thank you, God, for protecting us. For protecting Kelly. Please continue to watch over her.

The young woman was currently in surgery. The doctors were hopeful she'd make it. They surmised the icy temperatures in the mausoleum had spared her life by slowing her heart rate and lessening the bleeding from the single gunshot wound. It was difficult to know how long Kelly had been lying there. Hayley suspected it'd been at least overnight.

She breathed in the warm scent of Walker's laundry soap and felt the tension in her muscles ease. Hayley dipped her head back to look him in the face. He had a smudge of dirt on his cheek. She swiped at it. "You brought some of the cemetery back with you."

Walker caught her hand. "I didn't get a chance to say this earlier, but Hayley, I'm proud of you. So proud. Kelly has a fighting chance because you refused to give up on her."

The warmth tangled in his eyes undid her, as did the admiration in his voice. Walker lifted her up at every opportunity. Comforted her when she was hurting. Took pride in her strength. But Hayley wouldn't dare take all the credit for saving Kelly.

"*We* didn't give up on her." Hayley's hand splayed across the front of Walker's undershirt. His heartbeat was steady against her palm. "We make a good team, cowboy."

He smiled, and it erased some of the fatigue around his eyes. "Yeah, we do."

Desire unfurled inside her. Hayley rose on her tiptoes and kissed him. Heat burst through her, his touch doing more to warm her insides than any amount of coffee ever could. Under her palm, Walker's heart beat a rapid tempo. He pulled her closer and deepened the kiss. She molded against him, her hand trailing up to his neck, her fingers dipping into the soft ends of his hair.

She wanted this. Wanted him. Forever.

Her heart tumbled over and over with the realization. Could this be her future? It was both exhilarating and terrifying in equal measure. Walker was everything she'd ever dreamed of. Kind. Protective without being overbearing. Hardworking. She'd fallen in love with him at sixteen and never stopped, but before they discussed their future, they had to handle the threat.

When the kiss ended, Walker rested his forehead against hers. He was slightly breathless, and a feminine thrill raced through her. She'd done that. Unsettled this hard and tough Navy SEAL. She skimmed her fingers over the strong line of his jaw, the stubble scraping against her skin.

A throat cleared. Heat infused Hayley's cheeks as she glanced at the door to find Tucker standing with his back to them.

"Uh, sorry to interrupt"—Tucker glanced at them and did his best to suppress a smile and failed—"but Chief Garcia is ready to interview Aaron. He thought you two might want to sit in the observation room to watch."

Walker winked at Hayley and then took her hand. "Yes, we do."

Tucker led them to another room with a large-screen television hung on the wall. Electronic equipment was stacked on a desk nearby, along with a computer, all manned by an officer in uniform. Several loose chairs were scattered around the room.

Jason sat in the corner, drinking a coffee. Connor rested at his side.

Hayley greeted the dog with love and affection. "I heard you took down the big, bad sniper. What a good dog you are."

"Hold on." Tucker grabbed a chair, turned in backward, and straddled it before placing his arms on the back. "Connor didn't do it all by himself."

Jason cocked an eyebrow. "As I remember it, you were crouched behind a gravestone when the sniper was tackled."

"Yeah, cuz I was the distraction." Tucker scoffed. "Connor just bit the dude and dragged him into the grass." He pointed at his chest with an emphatic finger. "I'm the one who was shot at. It takes some serious gumption to be target practice for a criminal with a rifle."

"You weren't the only one being shot at." Walker rolled his eyes. "Stop being such a crybaby about it. He shot at me about half a dozen times right out there in the parking lot the other day. You don't see me asking for praise."

Hayley laughed at their brotherly bickering. "Okay, okay, I think we can say all of you were brave." Connor stared up at her with adoring brown eyes. She kissed the space between his brows. "But you most of all," she whispered.

Jason grinned at her and nodded in agreement.

The television on the wall flickered on. All the mirth evaporated from the room as Aaron Parker appeared on screen. He was slouched in a chair. Locks of greasy hair hung in his eyes. His clothes were grass-stained, his long-sleeved T-shirt ripped at the shoulder. A bandage peeked through the tear. Hayley surmised that was where Connor bit Aaron. She glanced at the criminal's shoes and her brows crept upward. He was wearing $400 sneakers.

Next to Aaron at the table was a man dressed in a suit. His lawyer, David Quinn. Chief Garcia was seated across from both of them. He went through the requirements of an interview, starting by reading Aaron his rights.

Hayley took a seat next to Walker, automatically reaching for his hand. His skin was warm, and he ran a thumb over the curve of her knuckles. She had the sense the connection meant as much to him as it did to her.

"Aaron." Chief Garcia folded his hands on top of the table. He appeared both authoritative and approachable at the same time. "You've been arrested for assault with a deadly weapon and attempted murder. That's serious jail time you're looking at. And that's before we get to the other charges. You've been quite busy."

David interjected before Aaron could answer. "What other charges?"

"Murder and kidnapping, for starters."

Aaron's face screwed up, and he slammed a hand down on the table. "I didn't do nothing. You can't prove I murdered anyone."

"Don't talk until I tell you to." The lawyer's tone was sharp. Then he turned to Chief Garcia. "My client has a point. What proof do you have linking him to any of those crimes?"

"Your client was using three former military veterans for target practice in the cemetery today right outside a mausoleum where a woman had been shot and left for dead." Chief Garcia focused on Aaron. "Kelly Fraser. That's the woman's name. Do you know what she said to a witness who gave her first aid? She identified her shooter as Casanova."

Aaron froze, and then his foot started bouncing up and down. He picked at a cuticle.

David set his pen down on the pad in front of him. "My client isn't Casanova."

"Oh, I already know that." Chief Garcia barely looked at David. All of his focus was on Aaron. "Aaron was a guest of the Harris County Jail on the night Kelly was kidnapped. But you know who Casanova is, don't you, Aaron? And it's a good thing you do because that means we can work out a deal."

Aaron's jaw locked. He dropped his hand to the table and glared at the chief. "I ain't telling you anything."

"He left you to be caught, Aaron. You're going to jail for a long time unless you help us. Is it really worth protecting him?"

A flare of anger sent heat rushing to Aaron's cheeks, staining them red. He leaned forward on the table until he was practically in the chief's face. "My brother is the only one who ever took care of me. We have a relationship you can't possibly understand."

Hayley inhaled sharply. "He's talking about Bobby Ray."

Walker grimaced. "Sounds like it."

Aaron smirked as if the chief was an idiot and then looked straight at the camera, as if he knew Hayley was in the observation room watching. Her gut clenched tight. The hatred in his eyes was palpable. It sent a wave of terror crashing over her because she knew exactly what message he was conveying.

This wasn't over. Not even close.

TWENTY-ONE

The night air was scented with wood smoke and damp grass. Walker breathed in deep, letting the cold sting his lungs. He checked the padlock on the building housing their tractors and then moved toward the barn. The horses were tucked in their stalls for the night. Midnight poked his head over the half-door to see who'd entered the space.

"Hey, boy. It's just me." Walker approached the huge animal and was encouraged when the horse nickered in greeting. A chuckle bubbled up as Walker stroked the horse's muzzle. "We're friends now, huh? I'm glad."

He lingered, showering attention on the horse before slipping out of the barn. Boone, ears flopping, raced across the yard to greet Walker. He patted the dog's head and received a lick on his wrist for the effort. An owl hooted. Several bats hunted in the pasture. The regular nocturnal activities of the animals eased the tension from Walker's muscles. There was a security system on the property. Hayley was safe.

But Walker couldn't shake the sense that Casanova was about to make his next move.

His gaze swept the area one last time, and then Walker headed up the path toward his house. Boone squeezed through the doorway ahead of him and jumped on Connor who was resting quietly in the corner. Jason worked on a laptop in the kitchen, a half-drunk cup of coffee at his elbow.

He glanced up. "Hey. Did you see the message from Nathan? He and your parents are on their way back from the doctor's office. They'll be here soon."

"I did."

Walker's dad had a scheduled X-ray that couldn't be put off. The doctor was concerned at his last checkup that the break wasn't healing properly. Surgery was in question. Nathan had accompanied Aileen and Shane to the appointment as a bodyguard. Walker trusted his friend implicitly but would breathe a sigh of relief once his parents were back on the ranch.

He crossed the room and poured himself a cup of coffee. How many did that make? Probably best not to think about it. Even now, Walker's eyes felt gritty. He hadn't slept well in days. Instead, he turned and gestured toward Jason's computer. "What are you working on?"

"Looking for Bobby Ray's hideout."

After interviewing Aaron, Chief Garcia sent a patrol unit to pick up Bobby Ray. The man was in the wind. No one could find him.

"Kyle is sitting outside Bobby Ray's apartment and Logan is at the Daniels property," Jason continued. "There's been no sign of him. I'm running through his friends and some of his old prison buddies." Jason lifted a shoulder. "Probably a waste of time since Chief Garcia issued a be-on-the-lookout for Bobby Ray. With every law enforcement officer in the state searching, Bobby Ray won't get far. But I figure every little bit helps."

"It does. Where's Hayley?"

"In the office going through the case files."

"I'll go check on her."

"Wait." Jason rose from the chair. He stood for a moment as if debating with himself and then looked Walker in the eye. "I'm not one to insert myself into things, but there's something I need to say. Especially now. We don't know what the next hour or even the next few minutes will bring."

Walker blinked. He leaned against the counter. "Okay."

"Tell Hayley you love her."

He stiffened. Walker was so caught off-guard he was momentarily speechless. He wasn't sure what surprised him more. That Jason had figured out how Walker felt about Hayley, or that he was giving unsolicited advice.

He dropped his gaze to his mug. "She's leaving. Hayley's been honest from the get-go. She has no intention of staying in Knoxville, and frankly, I don't blame her. This place holds nothing but difficult memories for her, and I'm a reminder of that. Lauren's death is a part of it. Casanova too. But it goes deeper than that. Hayley didn't have a good childhood. She deserves to leave this town behind and start fresh."

Jason didn't back down. "That doesn't change the fact that you love her."

"So what? It doesn't matter."

"It might." He scraped a hand through his hair and sighed. "You and I... all of us... we know how precious every breath is. And yet, we come up with all kinds of reasons to hold back. For me, it was my PTSD. For you, it's that Lauren's murder made everything messy between you and Hayley. It's understandable, but God has brought you together for a second chance. Don't let your fears mess it up."

Jason's observations were like a sucker punch. Walker flinched. "I'm protecting her."

"No, you aren't. That's just what you're telling yourself. I know from experience."

Walker studied his friend for a long moment. "You and Addison."

"Yep. I nearly missed out on having that wonderful woman in my life all because I was too scared." He straightened his shoulders. "I'm not saying Hayley will choose to stay. What I'm telling you is that she deserves to hear how you feel. Then she can decide what's right for her life."

There was wisdom in Jason's advice. Walker felt it sink into his heart and knew his friend was right. He nodded. "Thanks, man."

"Anytime, brother."

They shared a hug. Then Walker went down the hall to his office. He rounded the corner and his heart skipped a beat.

Hayley sat on the floor. She wore a sweater and jeans that skimmed her curves. Her hair was mussed from running her hands through it. Papers littered the carpet in organized chaos. Sophia, nestled in a carrier, slept a short distance away. Hayley's bare foot was extended, absently rocking the baby, as she read a report.

A swell rose in Walker's chest, so powerful and unstoppable, it almost bowled him over. He loved her. He loved her so much it was nearly painful. Hayley had stolen his heart when he was sixteen and she'd never given it back. There was no one else for him. "I love you."

Hayley glanced up from the report. She blinked and then her eyes widened as she registered what he'd said. Her mouth dropped open. "W-w-what?"

Heat flushed the back of his neck. Walker hadn't meant to say the words out loud, hadn't realized his mouth was moving, but maybe it was for the best. Fear had a way of closing things off and he didn't want to be scared of his feelings for her anymore. They were powerful. And wonderful.

Jason was right. Every breath was a gift, and they weren't guaranteed the next one. Walker had wasted enough time.

"I love you." He stepped into the room, setting his coffee mug on the desk, before reaching down to pull Hayley into a standing position. "There's a lot going on, but I don't want to let one more minute go by without telling you how I feel. I love you, Hayley Elizabeth

Barlow. I've loved you since I was sixteen years old. You were my first kiss, and if I have my wish, you'll be my last."

Tears flooded her eyes. "Is that a proposal?"

"It's a declaration. And a proposal, if you want it to be." He placed his hands on her waist. "The intention is not to pressure you into anything. Or even to have you say it back. I just wanted to let you know how I feel."

She wrapped her arms around his neck. "Well... in the spirit of saying our feelings, I'm in love with you too."

His heart stuttered like an old pickup and then took off like a bullet. Walker pulled her closer, his attention dropping to her beautiful lips.

He kissed her.

Everything in Hayley said this was right.

She leaned into Walker's kiss. Into his love. It was like stepping into sunshine after being in the dark for years. Brilliant and overwhelming and almost overpowering, but also warm and gentle. The old familiar prick of fear tried to shatter her happiness, but she refused to let it. Hayley had spent most of her life running scared. It was time to stop. To listen to the voice in her heart and trust God was leading her in the right direction.

The kiss ended, but Walker didn't pull away. His lips brushed against her mouth again. And then again. "I love you."

She would never tire of hearing him say it. "I love you too."

Walker's phone rang. He groaned.

Hayley laughed. "We had a few stolen moments of peace." She wriggled out of his arms. "Answer your phone. It's time to feed Sophia anyway."

The baby was awake and chewing on her fist. Yep, definitely bottle time. Hayley lifted Sophia from the carrier and tucked her into the crook of her elbow. The infant stared at her with wide eyes. A small crease formed between her brows as if she was trying to read Hayley's expressions. A tendril of warmth circled her heart.

Leah was right. Sophia was the most adorable thing.

"Okay, I'm putting you on speaker so Hayley can listen in. Hold on." Walker mouthed *Ryker* and then tapped on the phone screen. He followed Hayley down the hall and into the kitchen. "What did you find out about Aaron?"

"Nothing helpful. I've been rounding up gang members all afternoon, and while many of them had colorful things to tell me about Aaron, none of them knew he had a half-brother. His last known address is a homeless shelter. Aaron hasn't been there in months. From what I can tell, he's bounced around."

"That's not uncommon for guys like him."

Walker gestured for Hayley to hand him the baby so she could warm the bottle. She gently passed the baby off and kept listening as she moved around the kitchen.

"You're right," Ryker said. "It's not unusual, but it's strange no one knows Bobby Ray. I even tracked down several of Aaron's ex-girlfriends. One said Aaron mentioned a brother once and she even saw the guy from far away. I created a photo array and included Bobby Ray's picture. She didn't recognize him." Ryker's voice was laced with frustration. "I'm still digging, but I'm not certain Bobby Ray is the brother Aaron is talking about."

Walker's muscles tightened and he shared a glance with Hayley. "If it isn't, then we don't know Casanova's ID after all."

That was a terrifying thought. An unknown suspect was much harder to find.

She tapped some milk onto her wrist to check the temperature. "I have a hard time believing Bobby Ray isn't involved. He's missing."

"I can't explain that," Ryker said. "Maybe he got spooked. Chief Garcia dragged him down for questioning several times. After the experience with his dad, it's possible Bobby Ray got worried he was going to take the fall."

Ryker had a point, as much as Hayley hated to admit it. She gripped the bottle and had to force her fingers to relax. "We've searched state records. Thomas isn't listed as the father on anyone else's birth certificates."

"I'd start asking around town. If Thomas was cheating on his wife with multiple women, then people know about it. They also likely know which kids are his. At least, rumors will give you a jumping-off point."

Walker groaned. Hayley sympathized. Tracking down those leads would take time, which they didn't have. Casanova was planning something else. She could feel it.

Hayley gestured for Walker to hand her the phone. Maybe there was another lead that would help.

He exchanged the phone for the bottle and started feeding Sophia.

"Hey, Ryker." She leaned against the counter. "I was reviewing the files and found a minor note in Jessica Xavier's case." She'd been Casanova's second victim after Hayley escaped. "There was a surveillance video from a parking lot, but Casanova was wearing his mask and it was too grainy to make out other details. Do you know if they ever tried to clean it up?"

"I think the quality was too poor."

"Mind sending it over anyway. I'd like to look at it."

It was a long shot, but maybe something in the video would trigger her memories of Casanova and bring them closer to solving the case. Hayley would try anything.

"Sure thing," Ryker said. "I'll send it to Walker's email in a few minutes."

"Appreciate it."

"Absolutely. You two take care. I'll be in touch soon."

Hayley sank into a kitchen chair, the day's events and Ryker's news catching up to her. She was exhausted. Every time they made progress, it was snatched away.

Her gaze drifted across the room. Walker was standing near the stove feeding Sophia. If the baby was adorable, watching the two of them together was captivating. Her lips curled into a smile. "You're good with her, cowboy. When did you get so comfortable with babies?"

"After I got out of the military, I wasn't in a good headspace. Deployments take a lot out of you. You see the worst of humanity in war." He paused, his gaze some place far away. Then he snapped back to the kitchen. "Anyway, Mom thought it would be beneficial for me to change up my environment. Do something out of my comfort zone. She had me volunteer at the church day care."

Hayley gave him a knowing look. "Your mom is one smart lady."

"I know." He glanced at Sophia. "It's hard to feel like the world is an awful place when you have a baby in your arms. Something about them makes you hopeful. At least, for me." Walker gave her a wry smile. "I also think my mom was hoping it would encourage me to settle down and get married."

"I'm surprised none of the single ladies in Knoxville snapped you up."

He met her gaze. "They couldn't. My heart was already taken."

Oh, this man. Hayley wanted to drown in the warmth of his eyes. She saw her future with him, here on this ranch, their children and grandchildren running in the yard. Happiness. Sheer happiness.

Her phone rang.

Like a bolt of lightning splicing an oak tree in half, the joyful image in Hayley's head disappeared. Her heart sank. She didn't need to glance at the caller ID to know who it was.

Casanova.

"Hello, sweetheart." His voice spilled from the speakers the moment she answered. "You shouldn't have hit me in the library. That was a mistake that you're going to pay for. It's taken some time, but I've figured out the best way to settle the score. You see, Walker's mom and dad had a little accident on the way home tonight."

Hayley froze. Her gaze flew to Walker. His expression had gone frighteningly cold. Warrior cold. This... this was the Navy SEAL mask he used in battle. She turned her attention back to the phone. "You're lying."

"You know me well enough by now to know I don't lie." There was a rustle of fabric. "Aileen, say hello."

"Hayley, don't listen to him—"

Her words cut off with a yelp, as though she'd been hit. Anger unlike anything Hayley had ever experienced roared through her. Every time she thought Casanova had pushed her beyond her breaking point, he found a new one. Red mist coated her vision. Her whole body heated as if it was in an inferno.

As impossible as it was, Walker's expression grew even more stony. Somewhere in the back of her mind, Hayley registered the back door opening. Jason came in, followed by Tucker and Leah. She took the baby.

"Of course, I could be persuaded to let Aileen live." Casanova chuckled. "You once offered yourself for Kelly. Are you willing to do the same for Aileen, sweetheart?"

"Without hesitation." She knew it was a trap. Hayley didn't care. This was Walker's *mother*. "Name the place."

"Old Miller Barn. You have five minutes or I'll kill her."

TWENTY-TWO

Old Miller Barn was an unused cowshed tucked among a grove of trees on a dirt road. The property had once been a petting zoo and fruit orchard, but the Millers passed away, leaving distant relatives to fight over the inheritance. Five years later, they were still arguing. The apple trees grew wild and the structures on the land slowly rotted.

Walker killed his headlights as he turned onto the dirt road. Casanova knew they were coming, but there was no need to announce the timing of their arrival. He tucked his truck between a pair of overgrown fruit trees and killed the engine, then glanced at his watch. One minute to spare.

He checked his cell. No email from Ryker yet. They hoped the video would provide Casanova's identity, so even if things went sideways, law enforcement would have a fighting chance at stopping him.

Hayley unholstered her handgun, removed the magazine and checked it before slamming it back into place and loading a round. Walker followed suit with his own weapon. A knife pressed against the skin on his right leg. Both of them wore bulletproof vests, thanks to Tucker, who had extras in his patrol vehicle. He was coordinating the law enforcement response. It would take time to get officers and deputies into position. Walker wasn't willing to wait. Not with his mom's life on the line.

"It's not too late for you to bail, Hayley." Walker had tried to dissuade her from joining them at his house, but failed. The stubborn woman. "You don't have to do this. Jason is circling from the other direction and Tucker is on his way with more law enforcement. I'm not going in alone."

"This is a trap. You know it and so do I. The best way to combat Casanova is by working as a team." She met his gaze in the darkness. It was too dim to read her expression, but he imagined her chin was jutted out with determination. "I'm a trained soldier. It's my job to protect the innocent. Casanova might've started this, but we're going to finish it."

Her steely strength reached right inside Walker and wrapped itself around his heart. "Yes, we are." He took her hand. "But there's one thing I have to say. No matter what happens tonight, I love you. That will always remain true."

The first rule of battle was to believe in victory, but Walker had been down a similar path with Hayley when Lauren was murdered. It destroyed their relationship. Cost them ten years. If things went left, and something happened to his mom, Walker didn't want Hayley to blame herself.

He couldn't lose them both. He just... couldn't.

Hayley's fingers brushed along his jawline a moment before she leaned over and lightly kissed him. "Thank you for saying that. I love you too and I'm making you a promise. No matter what happens, I'm done running from happiness. God speaks in the silence of our hearts. He's been shouting in mine. I was stubborn for too long, believing He must be mistaken. I wasn't good enough. Wasn't worthy of the love you wanted to give me."

His chest tightened as emotion closed his throat. He didn't know Hayley had been feeling that way. "Because of Lauren?"

"In large part. Also because of my childhood and my mom. It's all tangled up together. The point is, I was wrong. God doesn't make mistakes. He's brought us together and I'm ready to finally fully trust where He's leading me." Hayley's thumb scraped across the stubble on his jaw. "I want a life with you, Walker. Sitting on the front porch of the ranch in our matching rocking chairs, sipping sweet tea, and watching our kids play in the grass."

The image she painted was one he'd imagined himself. Walker licked his lips, his heart skipping several beats. "Is that a marriage proposal?"

She laughed. "Pretty sure you proposed first, cowboy."

He pulled her closer and brushed his lips against hers. She tasted sweet, like sunshine and goodness. Just a brief kiss, but his heart beat a rapid tune against his ribs. Hayley brought out all the best parts of him. He could live without her if he had to—had done it before—but Walker prayed the vision they'd painted for their lives would come to fruition. He couldn't see how this ended, but he trusted God would see them through.

Hayley pulled back, but Walker snagged her hand. He ran his thumb over the inside of her wrist. Over her tattoo. Lauren's favorite verse, Hebrews 11:1. "Now faith is confidence in what we hope for and assurance in what we do not see." He breathed out. "Lauren told me once that it means believing things are going to be okay, even when we can't see how it'll work out. I've struggled with that. After her death, my faith faltered, but now I understand what she meant. God is asking us to trust Him even when we don't understand why things happen or how good could come from it."

"Yes." She gently squeezed his hand. "Lauren was wise beyond her years. Her faith sparked my own and I'll always be grateful for everything she taught me."

It was a legacy worthy of his beautiful and bright sister. Walker had hunted Casanova, seeking justice for Lauren, hoping that it would fill the void inside him. But she didn't need justice. She was with God and at peace. Stopping Casanova now was about saving lives.

The emptiness inside Walker needed to be filled with faith. Nothing else would do it. That's what Lauren had known, had tried to teach him. Now he understood.

They were running out of time, but Walker couldn't go without saying a prayer. He bowed his head, still holding Hayley's hand. "God, we come to you with humble hearts, asking that You guide our movements. Use us as Your instruments to protect the innocent. Give us the strength and wisdom to do the right thing. We put our trust in You and the ultimate goodness You've promised. Amen."

"Amen." Hayley's voice was soft. "That was perfect." She kissed him one last time. "Now let's see who's gonna do it better. Navy SEAL, an Army grunt, or the Marine with the bomb dog."

Despite the grim situation, Walker's lips quirked. "My money's on Connor."

"Mine too."

His phone beeped with an incoming message. Ryker's email. Walker quickly accessed the video and tilted the phone so Hayley could see it as well. The camera overlooked a parking lot. The images were grainy. Black-and-white. Casanova's facial features were indistinguishable, thanks to his hoodie and mask. He strolled into the frame and then out.

Hayley gasped. "That's Richard Westbrook."

Walker whipped his head to look at her. "Are you sure?"

"Positive. I spent hours watching him walk across the classroom during algebra. He favors his left leg, does this weird hop when he steps." Her brow crinkled. "Show it to me one more time."

They watched the short video again and then Hayley nodded. "It's definitely Richard Westbrook. I can't explain it. I don't know how he's connected to Aaron, but I'm telling you. That's Richard."

Her certainty was good enough for him. Walker texted Tucker, letting him know. His watch beeped. Their five minute window was up. He darkened his cell phone screen, silenced his phone, and then clicked it off. Without pausing for a second, he kissed Hayley hard on the mouth before reaching for the door handle. "Time to catch a killer."

"Let's do it."

Darkness pressed around Walker as he maneuvered across the brush to the old cowshed. Hayley was to his right, several paces away. Moonlight glimmered on the field and building. A rusted tractor, tires flat, sat parked among overgrown weeds. No sign of Casanova or his mother. Walker held up a hand for Hayley and pointed to the tractor. She gave him the okay signal and leveled her weapon to provide cover.

Sweat beaded on his brow as he lowered to a crouch. The weight of his bulletproof vest was familiar from his military days. A tinge of fear prickled his scalp as an internal warning system blared, designed for his survival. Walker had been trained to ignore it. He bolted from the cover of the trees. Every step in the open put him at risk. Walker expected any moment for a gunshot to ring out.

It didn't. He slid next to the tractor, heart pounding, and surveyed the area. The tall grass next to the barn door was pressed down, as if a vehicle had driven on it recently. No one was on the building's roof. If Casanova and his mother were here, they were likely inside.

Walker signaled to Hayley, keeping his eyes on the barn, and his gun at the ready to provide cover. He felt rather than heard her crossing the field. She dropped beside him behind the tractor. He leaned close to her ear. The scent of her tropical shampoo teased his senses, sharpened by the danger before them. "Cover me. I'm going to the barn."

She nodded. Once again, Walker took a deep breath, ignored his own base instincts, and raced across the field to the barn door. He peeked through the slats. His heart stopped.

The inside was illuminated with candles. His mom was

standing on her tiptoes at the edge of the loft, her wrists bound behind her, a rope wrapped around her neck. If she lost her balance, she'd hang. Sweat poured down her face and soaked her shirt. Exhaustion and determination warred for control in the curve of her brow and the sharp press of her lips. With horror, he watched as one of her feet slipped slightly before she righted herself.

Walker had intended to circle the building and look for another way in, but didn't have time. He needed to get his mom down now.

He signaled to Hayley, and a second later, she joined him. Her sharp inhale of breath followed.

"Oh, sweetheart, you keep breaking the rules." Casanova's voice spilled from somewhere in the recesses of the barn. "Bringing Walker to the meetup was not part of the bargain when you offered to make a trade."

Where was he? Walker squinted in the dark, wishing he had a set of night-vision goggles. The building was deep and wide, designed to hold dozens of cattle. Parts of it were metal. Casanova's voice bounced off the hard surfaces and changed directions. He could be anywhere inside.

"It's over, Richard." Walker's voice carried through the darkness. "The police know who you are and they're on the way. Turn yourself in and we can end this before anyone else gets hurt."

Silence followed. It was so deep and long, the night sounds returned. Wind rustled the trees and a small animal darted into the field before returning to the safety of the woods. Aileen clung to her balance, but her eyes had gone wide with Walker's declaration. A renewed determination creased her forehead, but she couldn't continue for much longer. Walker reached for the door handle. Hayley touched his back, indicating she was right behind him.

He peeled the door open to get a visual. A large metal barrel rested nearby and Walker pointed to it. Hayley nodded. She could use it as a shield while providing cover for him. Walker lifted three fingers. Then two, then one. He dashed through the barn door opening in a crouched position, his gaze fastened on his mom.

All at once, as if pushed by an invisible hand, several candles tilted over. A whoosh of heat followed as the pile of hay caught fire. Walker threw up a hand to protect his face. Aileen screamed and nearly lost her balance.

Casanova's laugh echoed around them. "Oops. Did I do that?"

Smoke filled the space at a rapid pace. The fire, fed by the hay, rapidly began licking at the edges of the loft platform. At Aileen's feet. The heat was intense, and she cried out.

Walker kept moving. The bottom rungs of the ladder leading to the loft were ablaze. He jumped over them, and ascended, desperate to get to his mom before she succumbed to the pain or fear and fell. Sweat coated his skin and the smoke burned his eyes. He held his breath, wading into smoke thick enough to hide a visual of the barn.

Hayley. Was she okay? Walker didn't have eyes on her, and that terrified him. The urge to give into that fear was overwhelming. Instead, he pushed it aside and focused on the mission. Getting to his mom.

Suddenly, she appeared in front of him. Walker shoved his gun into its holster and grabbed the knife from his boot before wrapping an arm around his mom's waist. He sliced through the rope. Aileen sagged against him. He lifted her into his arms and turned toward the ladder.

It was gone. Eaten by the flames. If Walker didn't find another way out of the loft, they were going to burn to death.

He spun around on his heel and aimed for the other side of the building. Aileen coughed violently. Her body felt frail and fragile in his arms, but his mom had an iron will. She'd keep fighting. It was a virtue she'd ingrained in both her children. Walker had forgotten for a while—let his grief get in the way—but Hayley had reminded him of the lesson. Hope always existed, even when things were bleak.

I trust in You, God. I trust in You.

Tears slid down his cheeks from the smoke. His throat burned as though he'd swallowed hot coals. Walker kept moving. His boots slid against the wood floor as a break in the fencing appeared. A ladder! He bolted for it and quickly descended.

A ghostly form emerged from the smoke. Walker's brain registered the enemy even before his consciousness fully recognized it. He dropped his mom's feet to the ground and shoved her behind him just as Casanova raised his gun.

The muzzle flashed.

TWENTY-THREE

A haze of pain clouded her thoughts.

Hayley groaned. Her head pulsed with the roar of her heartbeat, spreading agony along her scalp and down her neck. Her throat burned. She shifted, but her body wouldn't obey the command. Some internal warning system cut through the stabbing pressure in her head. Hayley cracked her eyes open.

The familiar scarred wood floor was immediately recognizable. Home. She was in her mom's house. Her jeans had been cut, socks and shoes removed. The bulletproof vest she'd been wearing was gone. Her long sleeves had been sliced off, revealing her arms from her shoulders down. Air washed over her bare arms and goose bumps followed. Her hands were behind her, tied together and secured to an old metal chair from her grandfather's work shed, dragged into the house by her mom years ago to use in the kitchen as a step stool.

Blood stained Hayley's shirt. Her muscles stiffened as flashes of memory assaulted her senses. Aileen struggling on the loft, Casanova tossing over the candles with some elaborate system made of fishing wire, and then the fire. Walker disappearing into the flames and smoke to save his mother. Hayley stood, intending to follow him, when Casanova came at her. She dodged the stun gun, nearly got a shot off, but the smoke blinded her. He'd come at her like a nightmare, tackling her to the ground. She hit her head on something hard. Passed out.

Then nothing.

A groan came from her left. Muscles protested as Hayley turned her head. Shock mingled with the adrenaline coursing through her system.

Bobby Ray.

He'd been badly beaten. A split lip and two black eyes fought for dominance over the bruises coating his cheeks. Like her, he was tied to a chair. His jeans had been sliced above the knees, his T-shirt ripped away to expose his arms. The sleeves dangled from his wrists, fabric bunching around his bindings. Hayley's concussion muddled her thoughts. She couldn't make sense of Bobby Ray's appearance. He groaned again, tried to lift his head, and then passed out.

The door behind Hayley opened, letting in a blast of cold air. That sudden wash of iciness drew attention to the warmth in the room. All at once, she noticed the crackle of flames and the scent of burning wood coming from the fireplace. Iron pokers jutted out. Just visible, deep in the fire, was the outline of a heart.

Hayley's breathing grew shallow as the brand on her shoulder burned with a fierceness that threatened to send her straight into a full-blown panic attack.

Footsteps whispered over the wood floor. Hayley's body trembled as she sensed him drawing near. A hand twirled a strand of her hair. Revulsion turned her stomach and bile rose in the back of her throat. She jerked her head away, the only resistance she could manage while tied to the chair.

Casanova chuckled and circled around to stand in front of her. The firelight reflected on the hard plastic of his white mask. "Obstinate to the end, huh, sweetheart?" He tsked. "If only you'd been compliant in the shed, like I told you to be. We could have avoided all of this."

Now that she'd seen the video, Hayley noticed other details that confirmed her identification of Casanova. A mole on the back of his hand. The slope and width of his shoulders. How could she not have noticed those before?

Hayley's fingers twisted to feel the binds at her wrist. She licked her chapped lips. Her mouth was so dry, but when her voice came, it was strong. "You kidnapped me and killed Lauren. News flash, Richard, that rarely gets you compliance."

He reared back and, faster than Hayley would've thought possible, backhanded her across the face. An explosion of agony temporarily blinded her as the chair tilted. Hayley slammed against the unyielding floor, the jolt sending another wave of pain through her body. The taste of copper filled her mouth.

Richard towered over her, his muscles rigid with rage. "Don't call me that. I'm Casanova."

He yanked the chair upright and got into her face. The plastic nose of his mask nearly touched her cheek. Beyond the dark cutouts for his eyes, the orbs of his irises drilled into her—same murky brown as Richard Westbrook's, there was no doubt—but the savageness lurking in their depths stole Hayley's breath.

"I'm Casanova," he repeated, his tone emphatic. "You will address me as such."

He backed away as suddenly as he'd come at her. Hayley's muscles involuntarily trembled. She swallowed and struggled to regain control of her terror and pain. Panic wouldn't help her. She knew that. As a soldier, she'd been trained to live with fear. To use it. But Hayley was trapped in a scene straight from her nightmares. A childhood trauma embedded so deep into her psyche, the reaction was automatic. It took every ounce of her training to engage the reasoning part of her brain.

To survive, Hayley needed to get untied.

She pulled a breath into her lungs. Then another. Her fingers found the edges of her binds. Zip ties. He'd used the same the first time he captured her. The plastic was strong, and the ties secured her hands together and then to the chair. They would be impossible to break with her body weight. Her mind started flipping through possibilities. Breaking the chair wasn't an option. It was metal.

Wait. Hayley's mind flashed to one of the few memories she had of her grandfather. He'd been a kind white-haired man with a big laugh and huge belly. She must've been four. Hanging out with him in his work shed. She scraped her finger on a broken, jagged piece on the back of the chair.

Was it possible... Hayley swallowed hard, her fingers searching the area. "Why did you bring me here?"

"Why not? It's rural and empty. No one will look for you here."

He was right. They were searching for Richard and Bobby Ray. No one would consider coming to her old house. The location was perfect for his purposes. Torture. Murder. Hayley's gaze locked on the poker heating in the flames. "The police know who you are. It's only a matter of time before you're caught."

Casanova ambled to the fire. "You think I haven't planned for that contingency?" He removed a glove from his back pocket and tugged it over his right hand. Reached for the poker. "Sweetheart, don't you know me by now? I plan everything."

"Was Aaron getting caught part of your plan?"

His muscles stiffened, just enough to let Hayley know that it hadn't been. "Aaron knew the risks. He agreed to them."

Her finger touched the jagged part of the metal. Yes! A prayer of thanksgiving lifted automatically. Hayley kept the excitement from her expression as she attempted to maneuver her wrists into position. "Do you honestly think he'll keep your secrets? Aaron is looking at life in prison. He can make a deal and get out in far less time."

"He won't turn on me." Casanova removed the poker from the

fire. The heart glowed red. "The only good thing I can say about our father is that he taught his sons loyalty to family always comes first."

Hayley froze. Her gaze shot from Casanova to the man tied to the chair next to her. Bobby Ray was awake now. His swollen eyes slitted open as far as he could probably manage. His body was stiff and hatred seemed to ooze from every pore of his body.

Suddenly, pieces that hadn't made sense snapped into place. She blinked. "You're half-brothers."

"Yes, sweetheart." Casanova twirled the poker. "I'm the eldest, born before my father married that sad sack of a woman who gave birth to this pathetic waste of humanity. Grew up in San Antonio, but my father often visited when I was a child. Once he brought a young Bobby Ray. We didn't get along."

In a blink, Casanova crossed the room and pressed the brand into Bobby Ray's thigh.

He screamed.

Hayley's own heart-shaped scar burned in response. Anger flowed through her, heightening her senses. There was no reasoning with Casanova. He was beyond any kind of logic. The only way to stop this was to get free. She squeezed her eyes shut to block out the horror show in front of her and focused on angling her wrists against the jagged piece of the chair. She sawed back and forth. The metal cut her skin. Blood trickled down her fingers.

Casanova removed the brand from Bobby Ray's leg. "You shouldn't have meddled in my plans."

Bobby Ray panted, his face contorted with so much pain, he couldn't reply.

Hayley froze as Casanova's gaze drifted to her. He studied her for a long moment and then ambled back to the fireplace. She breathed out and began working the binds again. "I don't understand. How did Bobby Ray meddle in your plans?"

"He threatened to out me if I didn't stop. Seems my baby brother had a change of heart in prison. He wanted to live a quiet life without crime."

"He knew you were Casanova."

"Not initially." He shoved the poker back into the fire. "Thomas left a suicide note confessing what I'd done and begging forgiveness from his wife. Dear old dad couldn't understand the beauty of my persona."

"Why didn't Regina turn you in?"

"Because I threatened to kill her." He shrugged. "Regina had no proof other than Thomas's letter, and by then, I'd proven what I was capable of. She was wisely convinced to keep her mouth shut. Until I started coming after you again. Then Regina told Bobby Ray. I captured him before he got to the police and now here we are." He fixed his gaze on her again. "You're asking the wrong questions, sweetheart. Don't you want to know why? Why I chose you?"

She was so close to sawing through the zip ties. Just a bit more... Hayley didn't care why, but she had to keep him talking. "Why?"

"Because you're a survivor, like me. From the moment you walked into high school, I knew you were something special." He twirled the poker in the fire. "But then you started following Walker around like a puppy. Flashing your smiles at him, sharing kisses. You were pure and perfect before he came along and soiled you. I had to take you from him. Once you were mine, you'd understand I was better."

It hadn't worked. She'd escaped the shed, and then his obsession turned to rage. "You forgot about me until I returned to town."

"Nooooo." He drew the word out, long and low, tinged with a made-up drawl that belonged to his persona. "I never forgot about you. I worked hard to perfect my craft."

"By killing others." Hayley's chest tightened as she pictured the photographs of the women pinned to Walker's corkboard. Innocent victims. "What did you do with their bodies?" She kept sawing at the zip ties. Almost there. "Did you bury them on the Daniels's property?"

It was the only thing that made sense. Richard had threatened to kill Regina Daniels if she revealed his identity. She was terrified. Turned a blind eye to what he was doing on the property. Bobby Ray was in and out of jail. Richard had the perfect setup.

"Of course." He removed the poker and checked the end. Seemingly dissatisfied with the temperature of the metal, he stuffed it back into the fireplace. Sparks flew. "Then once I had everything right, I brought you back so we could finish what we started."

Hayley's heart dropped to her stomach and then bounced back to her throat. "My mom died. That's what brought me to Knoxville."

"I know." His tone was casual, his attention on the fire. "Murder by overdose is a very simple thing to accomplish when the victim is a known drug addict."

The room spun and whirled as Hayley's world upended. Tears sprang, hot and fast, burning her eyelids with their intensity. She couldn't speak past the lump in her throat. Her mother had been murdered. The horror of what he'd done sank into her with fierce claws. She used it to fuel her movements. To get free.

The zip tie snapped.

Hayley froze as Casanova turned to face her. He pulled the red-hot poker out of the fire. "You disobeyed me, sweetheart, and I needed to teach you a lesson. Starting with your mother." He twirled the poker in his gloved hand. "And ending with Walker."

No! Not Walker. He wasn't dead. Couldn't be. Hayley rejected it with everything inside her. "You're lying."

"If only I were. Shot him as he tried to save his pitiful mother."

The rush of pain that followed his words was unlike anything Hayley had ever experienced. As if someone had reached inside her body and torn her heart in two. Tears ran unbidden down her cheeks.

Then some tiny, quiet part of her whispered that not all hope was lost. Walker was an ex-SEAL. He'd been injured in combat and come out the other side. She wouldn't believe he was dead until there was proof. Casanova's word was useless.

He ambled toward her. "You see, sweetheart, Walker didn't protect you. Because he doesn't love you. He can't."

The poker was angled toward her leg. Hayley flinched, as he expected her to.

Come closer. A bit closer.

He took another step toward her. Then another. "No one will ever care about you the way I do. You belong to me."

"Wrong." Hayley met his gaze. "I belong to God."

She sprang from the chair and tackled him.

TWENTY-FOUR

They hit the floor in a tangle of limbs.

Hayley landed on top, her shoulder still embedded in Casanova's midsection, his body breaking her fall. The poker flew from his hands and banged into the television stand. She wasted no time in using what little upper hand she had. Hayley slammed an elbow into his throat. He gasped.

A fist slammed into her head, knocking her off-kilter. Spots danced in her vision. The concussion from the attack in the barn was catching up to her.

She rolled away. A hand clamped down on her foot, the grip strong enough to bruise bone. Hayley's heartbeat grew frantic. Her vision narrowed on the poker in front of her. The end still glowed red hot. Her shirtsleeves, cut away at the shoulders, dangled from her wrists. She used the fabric as a makeshift glove and wrapped her hand around the hot poker before whirling around and smashing it against the hand holding her foot.

He screamed. Casanova—No, she wouldn't call him that—Richard yanked his hand away, pulling it to his chest. Hayley's stomach threatened to revolt right there as the room spun one way

177

and then the other. She willed her body to swallow back the bite of bile. Struggled to her feet as Richard lunged for the gun in his waistband.

She swung the poker without thinking, smashing him in the face with the hot iron. He pitched sideways. His head made a sick sound as it hit the side of the fireplace. The Casanova mask flew off and landed on the floor.

Richard didn't move. He slumped against the brick, eyes closed.

Hayley sucked in a breath. Her muscles trembled and her knees threatened to give out. Was he dead? Training told her to check his pulse and then search him for weapons, but she couldn't bring herself to get near him. She snatched the gun from the floor. Her gaze swept the room, looking for anything to secure him with, but the room was bare bones.

Bobby Ray whimpered from his chair. The wound on his leg was swollen and angry. A surge of sympathy coursed through Hayley. According to Richard, his brother had been about to turn him into the police. Bobby Ray had done some bad things in his life, but he didn't deserve to be tied up and tortured.

"Hold on." Hayley stumbled into the kitchen, dragging the poker behind her.

A phone was attached to the wall. She lifted the receiver. No dial tone. Of course not. Her mother likely hadn't paid the bill in months. A ring of keys dangled from a peg.

Her mom's truck. The vehicle was in the shed.

Hayley snagged the keys, shoving them in her pocket, and then opened the silverware drawer. She grabbed a knife. A wave of dizziness threatened to overwhelm her, and she shut her eyes for a moment. The blackness beckoned. She refused to give in to it. Richard was down, but he might not stay that way. She and Bobby Ray had to get out of here. Get help.

Then she could sleep. For days. Weeks.

The image of Walker rose in her mind. A sob tightened her chest.

It mingled with the grief of losing her mother and bonded to the head injury threatening to submerge her. Hayley tightened her hand on the knife. Forced herself to focus. Now was not the time to fall apart.

God, give me strength. Give me wisdom. Help me keep it together long enough to save Bobby Ray and make sure Richard's victims are found so their families can have some measure of closure.

The prayer strengthened her. Hayley straightened and went back into the living room.

Her steps faltered.

Richard was gone. A blood stain marred the fireplace, a testament to his injury, but the man himself was gone. So was his mask. The front door hung open. Blackness yawned.

"He ran," Bobby Ray murmured, his voice thick. His nose was probably broken. Maybe his jaw too. It was the first words he'd spoken, and from the way his face contorted with pain, it hurt.

Hayley's heart took off like a rocket. She didn't believe for a second that Richard had simply given up and fled. He wasn't the kind. Something dark inside him had driven him to this point, despite all the risks. Richard wouldn't leave Knoxville until she was dead. No matter what it took.

Her fingers trembled as Hayley slipped the knife against the zip ties securing Bobby Ray. She sliced through them. "Come on. We have to get out of here."

Bobby Ray attempted to stand and nearly toppled over. Blood coated his features. Hayley wouldn't be surprised if he also had a concussion. Indecision warred within her, but it was short-lived. Bobby Ray would slow her down, but with Richard out there somewhere, working on a new plan, Hayley couldn't leave him. She didn't know if Richard would come back to finish off his half-brother before she could get help. It wasn't a risk worth taking.

She slipped one arm around his waist. "Lean on me. We've got to move."

Bobby Ray tilted his weight off his bad leg and they hobbled together toward the kitchen. Frigid darkness enveloped them as they went out the back door. Ice coated the grass. The shed glimmered in the moonlight. Not far. A dozen yards.

"Over there." Hayley pitched her voice low. "My mom has a truck inside. We can use it to get away."

Bobby Ray nodded. He attempted to pick up his pace, which Hayley appreciated. Her bare feet slid on the frosty blades of grass. The cold bit into her. Her teeth threatened to chatter. Goose bumps pebbled her skin, and the hair on the back of her neck quivered. Richard was out here. She could feel him. Her heart raced in response to the unknown terror.

She gripped Richard's gun in her hand. Would it even fire? She stupidly hadn't checked the magazine, her focus on freeing Bobby Ray and then getting away. Her fingers were frozen. She did her best to adjust her hold while still supporting Bobby Ray and continuing their forward momentum.

A shadow shifted from the corner of the shed. Hayley's hand jerked upward. She fired as Richard flew out of the darkness like something from a horror movie. Her shot missed him, her aim compromised by the scars from her old injury, the concussion to her head, and the cold. A pitchfork, taken from the rear of the shed, was in Richard's hand.

Before she could get off another shot, Bobby Ray growled. He stepped in front of Hayley and attempted to grab the pitchfork. Hayley shifted her position but couldn't shoot Richard without possibly hurting Bobby Ray. Her fingers were numb. Her aim was too uncertain to risk it.

The two men wrestled before Richard gained the upper hand, twisting the pitchfork into Bobby Ray's leg. The man screamed and grabbed for his brother as he toppled to the ground.

Now! She had a clear shot.

Hayley fired again. This time, her aim was true and Richard stumbled back. He roared with anger and pain. Then rushed her.

She pulled the trigger, but nothing happened. The gun was jammed.

He slammed into her with all the force of a linebacker. Hayley flew through the air and landed on the grass with a painful jolt. All the air fled from her lungs. Her head swam. She couldn't think. Couldn't move. Within seconds, Richard was on top of her. His hands wrapped around her throat. Hayley internally screamed, willing her body to do something, but it wouldn't cooperate.

He squeezed. The tightness in her chest grew until it narrowed her vision to his face. His mouth was twisted with rage, thin strands of hair sticking out in all directions, adding to a look of madness. His eyes were bright with furor. Her heart thundered, the roaring blocking out all sound. Richard said something, but it was muffled.

Suddenly, his head jerked up. Richard's weight flew off of her as something brown launched over Hayley's head.

She rolled, struggling to suck air in through her damaged windpipe. One breath. Two. It hurt. Movement surrounded her. Arms enveloped her, hauling her against a chest that was familiar and reassuring. Hayley blinked to clear the tears from her vision and Walker's face came into view. He cupped her cheek. His touch was gentle and everything she needed.

"Just breathe, Hails. Focus on breathing. Nice and slow. That's it."

She followed his example until some of the tightness in her chest eased. The spots dancing in front of her eyes disappeared. Hayley touched his stubbled cheek. "You're... alive." If breathing hurt, talking was worse. She didn't care. "He said..."

"He lied. Bulletproof vest saved the day." Walker brushed a kiss on her mouth. Just a sweep of his lips, but it was like bathing in warm rain. "My mom is okay too. Both my parents are, along with Nathan. We're all okay. It's over."

She glanced over her shoulder.

Connor stood over Richard. The dog's mouth was open, his lips pulled back in a snarl, as he hovered over the killer's throat. Richard was screaming something about calling the dog off.

Jason stood nearby, his gun drawn and pointed at the man. Tucker raced up with several other officers and sheriff's deputies. Once they were in position to secure Richard, Jason called off Connor. The German shepherd instantly backed up. He crossed to his master's side but kept snarling until Richard was hauled away, handcuffed to a gurney, screaming about being shot. Emergency personnel also provided first aid to Bobby Ray.

Logan arrived, carrying his medic's bag. Hayley held up a hand to stop him from approaching. Not yet.

She turned back to Walker. His arms were still holding her close. Hayley snuggled deeper into his embrace. "How did you know where to find me?"

"Once we realized you were missing, I studied a map of the area. We knew Richard hadn't taken you far because Tucker had wisely set up roadblocks around Old Miller Barn. There were a few possible properties, but I had a gut feeling Richard would bring you here. Your mom's house is rural and unoccupied. Jason and Connor came with me, fortunately. Connor runs faster than any of us and he's scary enough to bring the worst criminals down. No one enjoys having a mad dog hovering over their throat." His mouth brushed against her temple and he breathed in deep. "Thank God, you're okay. Those were the longest and worst minutes of my life. I love you, Hails."

"I love you too." She touched his face, relished in the love she found in his eyes. Despite all her injuries, she smiled. "In the end, we were right. Connor was the one to bet on."

Walker roared with laughter.

Connor came up and licked Hayley's face. She rubbed the dog's fur for a moment, but then Walker stood, still holding her in his arms. "You look ready to pass out, Hails. Let Logan take care of you."

She held onto him. "You'll stay close."

"I'm not going anywhere."

TWENTY-FIVE

Walker opened the passenger-side door of his truck and held out a hand toward Hayley. She slid her fingers against his palm. Warmth coursed through him at the simple touch.

It'd been three days since Richard Westbrook's attack on Hayley. She'd spent a day in the hospital under observation for a concussion and, after being released, had stayed on Blue Star Ranch. Sleep and homemade food returned the color to her cheeks. Her silky hair covered the stitches in her scalp caused by hitting her head on cement in Old Miller Barn. Anyone looking at her would never have guessed she'd nearly died.

But Walker would never forget.

The time between discovering Hayley was missing and having her back in his arms were the worst minutes of his life. He said a silent prayer to thank God again for His loving protection. The events of the past two weeks had deepened his faith, and Walker vowed to keep it that way.

Hayley shot a nervous look toward the Knoxville Police Department as she stepped off the truck's runner and onto the ground. They had a meeting with Chief Garcia to discuss the aftermath of Richard's arrest.

Walker hesitated, his hand on the truck door. "We don't have to do this today. No one would blame you for putting it off for another couple of weeks."

She offered him a grateful smile and squeezed his hand. "No, I'm ready to put all of this behind me. It seems fitting to do this now before the barbecue at your house this afternoon."

Aileen, fully recovered from her injuries, was throwing a gratitude party. Family, Walker's friends, and members of the Knoxville Police Department were coming. Walker thought it was an excellent idea. They'd survived a harrowing ordeal. It was a welcome change to have something happy to look forward to.

Still holding hands, Hayley and Walker entered the police department. A few minutes later, they were seated in the visitor's chairs across from Chief Garcia. His uniform was ironed and crisp, but dark circles shadowed the skin under his eyes and exhaustion tugged his shoulders down as he sat in the large leather chair behind his desk. A hat impression pressed into the gray-and-brown hair at his temple.

"I'm glad to see both of you." The chief's gaze landed on Hayley. His expression was warm. "First, let me ask, how are you feeling?"

"Much better, thank you, sir." She absently touched the stitches hiding in her hair. The scars from her old bullet wound were red against the otherwise creamy skin on her hand. "I have another few weeks before the stitches come out. The doctor warned me to not whack my head again before the concussion fully heals." Hayley dropped her hand, a wry smile on her face. "So no horseback riding for a while. And I'm not supposed to hunt down any more serial killers."

The chief laughed. "Let's hope none of us have to do that." His expression grew serious as he shook his head. "This town owes you two a debt of gratitude for sticking with the case and uncovering what was going on."

Walker took Hayley's hand again. "We didn't do it by ourselves, sir. Solid teamwork brought Richard down, and I'm grateful to you for supporting us every step of the way. You're running a small police department and that comes with limitations and issues, but no one could ever accuse you of not doing your best for Knoxville."

Chief Garcia was quiet for a moment, seemingly overcome with emotion. Then he cleared his throat. "Thank you for saying that, Walker. It's been a rough few weeks, and the last couple of days have been even worse." He sighed. "Cadaver dogs searched Regina Daniels's property. We recovered the bodies of ten women buried in the woods."

Walker wasn't surprised by the news, but it made his heart ache all the same. "I only knew about eight."

"Two hadn't been reported missing because they'd disconnected from family before." Chief Garcia steepled his hands. "Based on the evidence against him, Richard pled guilty to avoid the death penalty. He confessed to everything. There won't be a trial, so neither of you will have to testify."

"That's a relief." Hayley breathed out. She squeezed Walker's hand and then turned back to the chief. "Did Richard explain his plan? He was going to kill Bobby Ray and me, that much is certain. And then what? How did Richard think he was going to get away with it?"

"He'd created a contingency plan. Near the women's bodies, we found a tarp-covered sedan. If you remember, Richard sometimes carjacked his victims. After killing them, he'd drive their car to a chop shop in Houston. It's owned and operated by a member of the same gang Aaron was involved in. At some point, Richard bought a sedan from the same place. There was a go-bag with a pile of cash and a fake ID in the trunk. He intended to start over with a new life."

"Leaving his wife and daughter?"

The chief nodded. "Neither of them had any idea he was Casanova. They were devastated to find out."

Walker leaned forward. "How did Richard explain his trips out of town?"

"Tutoring sessions for students of wealthy parents. Richard told his wife he had a set of steady clients. The story made sense when he'd show back up at home with a pile of cash—money which had actually come from selling a victim's vehicle to the chop shop. His wife didn't think to question it." Chief Garcia rubbed a hand over his face, then reached for a coffee mug at the corner of his desk. "I've searched through phone records, bank statements, talked to friends and family... I believe Richard's wife is telling the truth."

Hayley nodded. "It was part of his cover. A high school principal, a loving husband and father. No one suspected him of being Casanova, which was the point. Honestly, I'm surprised he told Aaron. That strikes me as risky."

"He used his brother to help him get rid of the victim's cars." Chief Garcia took a long drink of his coffee. "Aaron and Richard didn't grow up together, but they bonded once finding out Thomas was their dad. For some reason, Richard and Bobby Ray didn't get along so well. There was some kind of rivalry between them from the beginning." He set his mug down. "According to Richard, you were his first victim. He was obsessed with you. His plan was to keep you forever in the shed. On the day you were carjacked, Richard shoved a nail through Walker's tire to make sure he wouldn't show up at the school and stop the kidnapping."

Walker inhaled sharply as the chief's words gut punched him. "What? The flat tire I had that day was because of Richard?"

"Yes. He didn't know you were actually coming to the school to pick up Lauren. When Hayley offered her a ride home, it caught Richard off-guard. He stuck with the plan, but later said it was a stroke of good luck. He'd been wanting to get back at you for taking

Hayley's attention." The chief's gaze was sympathetic. "Killing Lauren was the way to do it."

A myriad of emotions whipped through Walker too quickly for him to process them all. He leaned over, propping his head in his hand as a rush of tears stung the back of his eyes. The intensity of his emotions surprised him. Walker knew he wasn't responsible for Lauren's death, but maybe, somewhere in the back of his mind, he'd still clung to the failure.

The sound of a chair scooting across the carpet came one moment before Hayley wrapped an arm around him. Walker wiped his eyes. He sat up, sheepish. "Sorry. That news hit me hard."

"No need to apologize, son. This case has hit all of us hard. Do you need a moment, or should I continue?"

"Go ahead." Walker wrapped an arm over Hayley's shoulders. He took a deep breath. "I'm okay."

"Richard's obsession with Hayley was mirrored by his hatred for you. After she escaped from the shed, he spent a few months considering his next moves. Thomas, his dad, surmised Richard was Casanova. The information ate him up, and he eventually committed suicide, leaving a note explaining to his wife Regina what happened. She confronted Richard with the news. He threatened to kill her if she said one word. Regina told us she was terrified of him. When Richard started showing up periodically on the property, she ignored it."

While Walker had some sympathy for Regina, it commingled with anger. "He was killing people. She knew about it and said nothing."

"She's been arrested as an accessory after the fact. I'm sure she'll get a plea deal, but Regina will have consequences for her actions. There were things she could've done to stop Richard a long time ago." Chief Garcia scraped a hand through his hair. "Years went by while Richard periodically kidnapped and killed different women. Practicing, he called it."

Hayley's mouth tightened. "Richard was planning on coming after me for a long time. Ten years." Her voice cracked. "He killed my mother to bring me back home."

Walker hugged her tighter. Their grief was painful, but sharing it made the burden easier.

The chief nodded. "The ten-year anniversary was a trigger for him. And yes, he got some drugs from Aaron and injected your mother with them to cause an OD. Her death certificate will be changed to reflect the cause of death. Richard will plead guilty to her murder. I know it's small consolation, but I hope it gives you some measure of peace."

"It does. Thank you."

"Richard had a whole plan laid out. He killed Julianna, so you'd show up at the school. He wanted to interact with you. The phone calls, the notes... all of it was designed to mentally distress both you and Walker. The attack on the library was carried out by Richard and Aaron."

"Yeah, that was confusing. Richard was in the library with us, picking up his daughter. How did he get back so quickly?"

"Her piano lesson is one block over. He dropped her off and came back, met up with Aaron, who had escaped from Walker, and then attacked the library. Richard intended to kidnap you, which would have the effect of causing Walker to spiral into a panic. He would trace the note to the mausoleum and then Aaron would kill him. Things went awry when you escaped, Hayley. Then Aaron was captured. It left Richard scrambling."

Walker grimaced. "That's when he kidnapped my mom."

The chief nodded. "Before he could, Bobby Ray found out from his mom what was really going on. He was coming to the police station when Richard captured him. He held Bobby Ray at Hayley's house, beating and torturing him. Originally, he was going to frame Bobby Ray for the murders, but once he knew the police were aware of him, Richard decided to kill his brother. Hayley too. Then he'd escape town." Chief Garcia shook his head. "It's scary to think how close he came to getting away with it."

Walker agreed. "What about Kelly? Will she be all right?"

"Doctors say she'll make a full recovery. In fact, Kelly asked if you would stop by to visit her. She'd like to meet you both."

"I'd like that too." Hayley leaned against Walker. "I'm glad this is over. I want to put this chapter of my life behind me."

"I don't blame you one bit." He held up a finger. "There's one more thing I want to discuss before y'all go. Actually, with you, Hayley. I don't know what your plans are, but there's a position here at the police department for you, should you want it."

Her mouth gaped open for a moment. "But... I can't pass the firearm exam—"

"Tucker explained your injury. The position isn't for an officer." He waved at the paperwork scattered on his credenza nearby. "I need support personnel. Something akin to a chief deputy. You won't be expected to carry a firearm or go out on patrol, but you'll keep on top of the paperwork, coordinate the officers, and assist on cases as needed. Your experience in working investigations would prove invaluable. I have green officers who need someone to guide them."

Hayley was quiet for a long moment, and then a smile crept across her face. "That sounds like something I would be interested in. Very interested."

The chief's shoulders dropped in relief. "I was hoping you would say that. To be fair, I did some digging into your background, and your superior officers had amazing things to say about you. We can talk logistics another day, but I'd be thrilled to make you a member of the department."

"Thank you for thinking of me, sir."

They all rose. Chief Garcia shook Hayley's hand warmly before doing the same to Walker. "Your mom told me about the barbecue this afternoon. I'll drop by soon."

"See you then." Walker gave a last wave as he and Hayley left the office.

Cold air smacked his face as they exited the police department, but the sunshine eased some of the bite. Walker lifted his face toward the sky. He breathed in the crisp air. It renewed him, easing the last of the tension from his muscles. He stopped next to his truck and pulled Hayley into his arms. Everything about having her near felt right.

Hayley wrapped her arms around his waist. "You okay?"

"I feel about ten pounds lighter than when I entered. You?"

"The same." She bounced on the balls of her feet and grinned. "I can't believe he offered me a job. It sounds perfect, doesn't it?"

"It does." Walker matched her smile and then kissed her forehead. They hadn't discussed their relationship since the attack, but the love between them had only grown stronger in the last few days. Since they were clearing the decks today, it seemed an appropriate time to make his intentions toward Hayley crystal clear. "The barbecue kicks off in an hour, but there's someplace I'd like to take you first. Would that be okay?"

"Sure." She tilted her head. "Where are we going?"

"You'll see."

TWENTY-SIX

Twenty minutes later, Hayley's tennis shoes crunched against the small gravel on a secret path on the far side of Blue Star Ranch. Sunshine filtered through the trees, dappling on the ground. A squirrel darted across the path before scurrying up a pine. Birds chirped overhead. Hayley hung her finger through the belt loop on Walker's pants. Her arm was around his waist, his slung over her shoulders. They walked in lockstep.

"I'd forgotten how beautiful this part of the ranch is." Hayley smiled up at Walker. The sight of him made her heart skitter. His jaw was peppered with a five-o'clock shadow, his cowboy hat perfectly placed on his head. Coupled with the Wranglers, beat-up leather jacket, and dusty boots, he could've graced the cover of a romance book about cowboys. But it was more than his looks that touched her heart. It was his bravery and steadfastness. The way he loved his family. The way he loved her.

Walker returned her smile. "It's been a long time since I've come down here myself."

She didn't need to ask why. This was their special place. Their secret spot. While dating in high school, she and Walker used to ride their horses down this path. Bring their school books and a blanket on pretty days and do homework under the shade of the trees. In the spring, the meadow was full of flowers.

They rounded a bend in the path and the trees parted. A picnic bench rested in the clearing. Pine needles and leaves covered its surface. Hayley's heart leapt for joy as the carving embedded in the bark of a nearby oak tree came into view. Tears filmed her eyes. She dropped her arm from around Walker's waist and crossed to the tree. Her fingers trailed over the letters inside the crudely drawn heart.

WM + HB

"I used to dream of this place." Her voice was soft as the memories of their sweet romance unfolded in her mind. The kisses, the laughter, the teasing way Walker stole her candy while they were studying. "It was the one place I could conjure in my mind that could make my heart lighter."

It wasn't just the beauty of the nature surrounding them. It'd been Walker that infused this special place with joy. Here, Hayley had been free. She could forget about everything going on at home and just be... her.

"It was the same for me." Walker came up behind her. His hand touched her back. "There were long nights while I was on deployments. Times I couldn't sleep or when my mind wouldn't shut off. This is the place I would think of. This place. And you." He dropped his hand. "Which is why I wanted to come here to do this."

Hayley turned and inhaled sharply.

Walker was down on one knee, a jewelry box open in his hand, an engagement ring nestled inside. The diamond sparkled in the sunlight. "I love you, Hails. I want to build a life with you, the one we talked about, and I don't want to wait one more minute to start it. Please marry me."

The tears filming her eyes spilled over onto her cheeks. She grabbed his wrists and pulled him into a standing position before throwing her arms around his neck. "Yes, Walker. Yes, I'll marry you."

Walker captured her lips with his. The outside world ceased to exist. Hayley's existence narrowed to the man holding her tenderly in his arms and the feelings tumbling through her. Here, with him, she was whole. Perfect. Loved. She couldn't have asked God for a more beautiful moment.

The kiss ended. Hayley was breathless with the force of her emotions. Walker removed the diamond ring from the box and slid it on to her finger. Then he lifted her hand to brush a kiss across her knuckles. "You've made me the happiest man on earth, Hails."

She pulled him closer. "You know, you'd already proposed. It wasn't necessary to do it a second time."

He brushed a strand of hair from her face. "You deserve a proper proposal. A memory that holds only joy and happiness." Worry crept into his expression. "Did I do okay?"

Her heart squeezed tight. "You did more than okay, cowboy. It was perfect. I love you."

"I love you too."

Walker was on top of the world when he opened the front door to his parents' house. The scent of macaroni-and-cheese mingled with baked bread and a hint of something chocolate. Boone rushed to greet them, running right past Walker and straight to Hayley. The hound sat at her feet, but his hind end wriggled with excitement.

Walker planted his hands on his hips. "You're supposed to be my dog."

Hayley laughed and bent down to lavish the mutt with affection. "Wrong, cowboy. Now he's our dog." She rubbed his ears. "And don't you know it, Boone? Yes, you do." She planted a kiss between the dog's brows.

Our dog. Walker loved the sound of that. He snagged Hayley's hand and drew her close for a kiss. The taste of her lips was intoxicating.

She gave him a slight shove, her cheeks turning pink. "Keep it PG. We're in your parents' home."

He laughed. "Once they see we're engaged, they won't care how many kisses we share in the entryway. My mom's going to be counting the days until our wedding, and the minute we walk down the aisle, she'll be after us for grandbabies." Walker wiggled his brows. "I hope you know what you've gotten yourself in to."

That sweet flush on her cheeks deepened, and a smile played on her lips. "Grandbabies, huh? I hope you know what *you've* gotten *yourself* into. I want a dozen."

That made him roar with laughter. "Whenever you're ready for babies, I am." Walker kissed her again, light and flirty, but full of love. "I meant what I said. I'm ready to start our lives together. We could get married today, if you wanted. I'm committed to you, Hails."

She chuckled. "Not today." Hayley winked. "We have a barbecue."

The sound of voices filtered from the kitchen. Walker grinned and kept hold of Hayley's hand, excitement building as he anticipated how happy his parents were going to be with the news of their engagement.

The scene that greeted him when he walked around the corner gave Walker pause. His dad was seated at the table, cast propped up on a chair. Aileen stood behind him, one hand on his shoulder. Tear tracks ran down her cheeks and she clutched a tissue.

Across the kitchen, Leah was sobbing in Tucker's chest. He cupped the back of her head lovingly, his other arm wrapped around her waist. Sophia was nestled between their bodies, held in Leah's arms. The baby was sleeping peacefully.

"What happened?" Walker's gaze shot around the room. He glanced at Hayley, who looked equally confused. The joy of their engagement leached from his insides until they were wrung out. "How bad is it?"

"The social worker came by." Aileen swiped at her tear tracks. "She located Julianna's family. Her extended cousins in Wisconsin."

Walker closed his eyes. No wonder Leah was sobbing. She'd become very attached to Sophia, and it was going to be devastating to say goodbye. As a cancer survivor, she couldn't have kids of her own and Walker knew they'd been going through the adoption process. This was a blow. "The family decided to take her?"

Aileen shook her head. "No."

He frowned. "Then...?" Walker met Tucker's gaze with a questioning glance, hope springing in his chest.

Leah sucked in a deep breath and lifted her head from Tucker's chest. She removed her glasses and swiped at the tears on her cheeks. "We're adopting Sophia." Her chin wobbled. "She's going to be our daughter." She laughed. "I can't believe I just said that."

Tucker nodded. "We've been going through the process for a while. Home visits with social workers and working with different agencies. Nothing was going as planned. But then Sophia arrived..." He kept an arm around Leah's waist as he looked down at the baby. "She stole our hearts."

Walker whooped quietly to avoid waking the sleeping baby, and then he embraced Tucker in a brotherly hug before kissing Leah's cheek. The couple had been through rough times together, but had gotten through them with love and faith. They deserved all the happiness life had to offer.

Hayley stepped forward to hug Leah. "Congratulations. I'm so happy for you both."

"Thanks." Leah bit her lip. "I want you to know that we're going to make sure Sophia understands her birth parents loved her very much—"

"Of course you will." Hayley gave her a warm smile. "You're going to make a wonderful mom. What happened is tragic, but this is God's way of having something good come out of the bad. Sophia is blessed to have so much love surrounding her."

"Thank you, Hayley. That's sweet of you to say." Leah smiled, and it lit up her whole face. "I'm going to be a mom. I can hardly—" Her eyes widened, and she grabbed Hayley's left hand. "Oh, wow!"

Aileen yelped and her hands flew to her mouth. "Are you two engaged?"

Walker chuckled and then nodded. "We have a lot to celebrate this afternoon."

There was another round of hugs and more tears. Even Walker's dad was misty-eyed.

Moments later, the front door opened and Jason hollered a hello. He entered the kitchen carrying a stack of pie boxes from Nelson's Diner. His wife Addison, her long hair tucked in a ponytail, followed behind. Her T-shirt stretched over the slight baby bump forming at her midsection. She and Jason had recently found out they were having a little boy. More hugs and tears followed as everyone shared their news.

Half an hour later, the entire crew was scattered around the house. Kyle and his wife Sierra helped their son Daniel build a block tower while chatting with Cassie and Nathan in the living room. Logan and his wife, Willow, were in the kitchen preparing the burgers to be grilled under Aileen's supervision. Hayley bounced in time with the music playing on the speakers as she chopped veggies for a salad, a broad smile on her face. Her happiness was infectious. Walker kissed her cheek as he went by, breathing in the scent of her tropical shampoo.

Hayley's smile widened, which sent butterflies fluttering in his stomach. Walker wanted to linger in the kitchen with her, but more guests would arrive soon. He grabbed a plate of steaks and slipped out the back door. The meat sizzled as it hit the hot grill.

Logan bounced down the porch steps, holding two soft drinks. "Hold on, maybe you need to lower the temperature."

"Get out of here. Last time you manned the grill, the steaks were raw and the burgers burned." Walker waved the tongs. "I know what I'm doing."

Logan handed him a drink. "Sure, sure." He rolled his eyes. "You're the grill master."

"I am."

The back door opened again. Jason, Nathan, Kyle, and Tucker poured out of the house. All of them had soft drinks and all of them looked like they were ready to give an opinion about the grill. A fight always broke out whenever there was meat and a barbecue involved.

Walker groaned. "I don't need help from the peanut gallery." He waved his tongs. "All of you, go back inside."

"No can do. The ladies are talking about babies, diapers, and pregnancy." Nathan's eyes widened. "Did you know infants go through six to eight diapers a day?" He whacked Jason. "Dude, that's a lot of diaper changes coming your way."

Jason shoved him. "I'm sure Uncle Nathan will be happy to help."

They all laughed. Every one of them would take over babysitting duty. Their kids would be blessed with lots of aunts and uncles. While Walker wasn't blood related to these guys, they were family in every sense of the word.

He eyed his friends gathered around the grill. All of them married—or almost married in his case—some with kids already. Others with babies on the way. The future looked bright.

"Guys, I have to say thank you one more time." Walker clapped a hand on Jason's shoulder. "I couldn't have gotten through these past few years after deployment without you. And when Hayley was in danger, you all jumped in to help. I'm blessed to have y'all in my life."

"No need to thank us." Jason grinned. "That's what brothers do."

The guys hollered and whooped in agreement.

Walker raised his soda can. "To brotherhood."

The response was booming as they all raised their drinks. "To brotherhood."

ALSO BY LYNN SHANNON

Texas Ranger Heroes Series

Ranger Protection

Ranger Redemption

Ranger Courage

Ranger Faith

Ranger Honor

Ranger Justice

Triumph Over Adversity Series

Calculated Risk

Critical Error

Necessary Peril

Strategic Plan

Covert Mission

Tactical Force

Would you like to know when my next book is released? Or when my novels go on sale? It's easy. Subscribe to my newsletter at www. lynnshannon.com and all of the info will come straight to your inbox!

Reviews help readers find books. Please consider leaving a review at your favorite place of purchase or anywhere you discover new books. Thank you.